MINA

MINA

Kim Sagwa

Translated by Bruce and Ju-Chan Fulton

TWO LINES
PRESS

Originally published as: 미나 by Kim Sagwa
Copyright © 2008 by Kim Sagwa
Originally published in Korea by Changbi Publishers, Inc.
English edition is published in arrangement with Changbi Publishers, Inc.
All rights reserved.

Translation © 2018 by Bruce and Ju-Chan Fulton

Two Lines Press
582 Market Street, Suite 700, San Francisco, CA 94104
www.twolinespress.com

ISBN 978-1-931883-74-0

Library of Congress Control Number: 2018933968

Cover design by Gabriele Wilson
Cover photo by Gallery Stock
Typeset by Sloane | Samuel

Printed in the United States of America

1 3 5 7 9 10 8 6 4 2

This book is published with the support of the Literature Translation
Institute of Korea (LTI Korea) and is supported in part by an award
from the National Endowment for the Arts.

ART WORKS.
arts.gov

PART ONE

THE TRIO

"Minho," says Crystal. A right triangle of her fair cheek shows through the crack in the doorway.

"Crystal," says Minho.

Crystal darts inside and the door closes and locks with a three-note warble.

Crystal walks slowly toward the living room. Up tilts her head toward the ceiling. Sky. Chandelier. Dim light. She grins at Mina, her eyes narrowing to slits.

"Mina."

Mina is lying gracefully on the living room floor, hands folded over her stomach, eyes closed, her expression blissful. Kim Gordon's voice pours from the speakers: "*Wish I could change the way that you feel…*" Mina turns toward Crystal with a languid smile. Crystal watches as Mina is slowly but surely suffused with the beautiful sound. She looks up at the pair of speakers. They're stripped-down and bare— what passes for modern design. Crystal eases down onto Mina's chest and begins to strangle her. Minho turns off the lights. Mina's face reddens, her eyes still closed. The sky dims. Crystal tightens her grip and Mina's face contorts, her mouth gaping. Minho, as always, is smiling. Gradually the three of them are enveloped by darkness. This is a game, a joke, it's not for real.

"Once upon a time there was a princess who had a passion for snakes. She pestered her father the king until he created a garden for her in the corner of the palace grounds, a garden of plants and trees and swarming snakes. One of those snakes she treasured above all the others, cherishing it like she would a crystal. The princess announced far and wide that she would kill herself if the snake died before she did. Then one day the snake disappeared. The princess ordered her ladies-in-waiting to find it. They each brought her a snake from the garden, but each time the princess shook her head, whereupon the lady would kill the snake and throw it into a deep pit. The other snakes began to disappear from the garden, some slithering off, others crawling high up in the trees. With bow and arrow the princess began to eliminate the remaining snakes, but she could not find the snake she loved. She wailed as she tried to decide whether to kill herself or disappear along with the snake. But how could she kill herself when she wasn't sure her snake was dead? And how could she vanish when her face was known to everyone? One day she came down with the flu. The end had come, she decided. She might hang on for a while but she was doomed to die. Saddened, the king had an exact replica of her snake carved from crystal and gave it to the princess. *Aha.* Ecstatic, the princess threw the crystal on the floor and it broke. With a long shard of the broken crystal she stabbed herself in the heart, inflicting a mortal wound. Her snake reappeared, coiling itself around her and licking her blood with its crimson tongue. The outraged king tried to kill the snake but instead was bitten and died from the venom. The snake slithered away, never to be seen again."

"That snake is me," Crystal says, releasing Mina's neck. Mina coughs violently. Minho turns the lights back on and a red mark resembling a slithering snake appears on Mina's fair neck. Crystal caresses it ever so gently. "Does it hurt?"

Mina shakes her head. "You'll have to do better than that if you want to kill me," she says with another loud cough.

"I guess I should have known better."

"Well, you do now."

"How was my story, anyway?"

"Stupid."

"Yeah. But it came from in here—it's yours, right?" Crystal shows Mina a hardcover book with a sky-blue jacket illustrated with the beautiful princess bleeding to death and the king glaring furiously at the snake coiled around his neck with its tongue extended.

"Who cares about kids' books?"

"Wow!" says Minho. "Where did you find *that*? Let me see."

"In your father's study."

"Is the snake really named Crystal?"

"No, I made that up."

"Dumbass."

Crystal looks around with a vacuous expression as if she's just awakened from a dream. Mina's head sways to the music. Crystal caresses Mina's hair, wrestling with an urge to strangle her again. Mina smiles a perfect smile.

"Happy?" says Crystal.

"About what?"

"About right now, this moment."

"Perfect."

"What's perfect?… I don't get it."

"You wouldn't," says Mina, looking at Crystal in disdain.

"Maybe not." Crystal sighs, gets off Mina, and lies down next to her. "Mina?"

"What do you want?"

"My mom gave me some money. Let's order in, I'm hungry." She turns and hugs Mina.

"How much have you got?" Mina snatches the money as soon as Crystal takes it out of her pocket.

"Spicy chicken for me!" Minho calls out.

"Fuck off!" Mina says. "I want pizza!"

Minho rummages through the DVDs in the bookcase without responding.

Crystal gives Mina a blank stare.

"Look close…do you think I'm bipolar?" asks Mina.

Crystal knows Mina has taken antidepressants and tranquilizers, been into Freud and Jung. Kim Gordon wails. Crystal takes Mina's hands. "No, not at all."

Mina frowns.

Minho calls in the pizza order. Mina, still lying on her back, chants, "Potato pizza, potato pizza." Crystal, humming innocently, stands up and goes for Minho's back pocket. Minho tries to dodge her but she's too quick. His wallet in hand, she scampers off giggling. Minho grabs her wrist and twists it, and the giggling turns into a burst of laughter. Minho twists harder and Crystal screams. She's still smiling. Mina is still lying on the floor, cold and uninvolved, her languid body producing a languid smile. Crystal and Minho, cheeks lit up by their smiles, gasp for breath. When Minho puts down the phone he lunges at Crystal. She falls to the floor, the wallet flies free, and Minho reaches for it. Crystal bites his finger. She grabs the wallet. Minho yanks at it. Back and forth they pull at the wallet. Crystal smirks at him. He pulls on the wallet for all he's worth and suddenly she lets go and Minho sprawls backward onto the floor clutching the wallet, his right elbow jabbing Mina in the thigh. Mina screams. Crystal and Minho look at each other with a *what's-up-with-her* expression. Mina screams louder. Crystal crawls to the CD player and cranks up the volume, overpowering Mina's screaming until it can no longer be heard. Mina stops screaming and crawls toward Minho.

"Tell me you're sorry—it's your fault, say it." Scowling, she displays her thigh.

Minho smiles. "Sorry."

"Son of a bitch. That hurt!"

"Sorry!"

"You son of a bitch. That *hurt*!"

"I'm sorry, really."

"You're still a son of a bitch…"

Minho just can't wipe the smile from his face. Mina gets angrier. Still Minho smiles. Crystal wags her finger in time with the music and watches them with a beatific smile.

"That's cute. You two are so lucky! So that's what it's like to have a sibling."

Mina and Minho look at each other and laugh, "Oh, we're *siblings*—awesome!"

"Stop it, you two. Don't laugh. Okay, I should have said *brother* or *sister*—so what?"

"Bro and Sis," says Minho. "What!" says Mina. She's rolling on the floor, laughing. "Bro and Sis? Bro and Sis—that's stupid!" She can't stop laughing. "Yuck!"

"Stop, don't make fun of me. Quit it!" Crystal covers her face and sprawls on the floor.

"Don't play coy," Mina says, yanking Crystal's hands from her face as Crystal bursts out laughing.

"Why are you laughing?"

"You tickled my face."

"Crazy bitch!"

"Minho, are we going to watch a movie or what?"

"Coming right up."

Minho turns on the projector and the dark wall comes alive. Mina lies down next to Crystal and the two of them start whispering. Minho taps Crystal on the shoulder and puts an index finger to his lips. Mina makes a face and bites her lip. On the wall, two women kiss passionately. Mina starts to nod off. Crystal gazes at Mina and then at Minho. Outside the sun is setting; inside, the wall on which the movie is projected surges toward her, dreamlike, then recedes. Eyes open or shut, it all feels like a dream. A woman is singing in a theater but her voice is inaudible; she collapses on the stage. Crystal is no longer watching. She's looking at the ceiling instead. *I wish I lived up there. Then I could come down here and play on this carpet.* The coffee-colored carpet on which she's spread is woven with an image of Venus, fair skin exposed, lying next to her lover. Crystal lying on the coffee-colored carpet imagines she's looking up at a vision of Crystal lying next to Venus in the clouds. The two Crystals hold their breath and regard each other. Everything freezes. From the speakers comes a song as the movie ends.

Yawning, Crystal rises and sweeps a large wooden brush through her hair. With a faint tremor of static electricity, wisps of hair rise and then settle. Minho turns on the light. Mina is caught in the act of rolling over while stuffing a slice of pizza in her mouth; the pizza has gone cold. Minho turns off the projector. There's a sudden silence. Minho and Crystal fall to the floor one after the other. The window is open a crack but not a breath of air comes through it. The prone trio forms a crooked isosceles triangle. Crystal yawns and lifts a leg. "Panties, Crystal," Mina reminds her. Crystal lowers her leg. The fog spreading outside has the same champagne color as the chandelier. Crystal is enthralled by the geometric pattern on the ceiling—spiraling ovals and diamonds funneled into a wedge. "Coffee-colored carpet," Crystal murmurs. "What?" says Mina. "Coffee-colored carpet...." Mina lurches, closes the window, returns to her place on the floor, and stretches out the same as before. "Minho, music please." "I don't want to." "But I don't want to get up." "Why?" "I'm paralyzed." The lazy quiescence of the late afternoon lingers. Minho stuffs the last chicken wing into his mouth. "Tastes like shit."

"Idiot—you only realize that after scarfing down the whole thing?"

"You're dead, Kim Mina."

Crystal's cellphone rings. "Hello?"

"You love M, don't you?"

It's a morose and testy voice she doesn't recognize.

"Hello?"

"You there?"

"Hello—who *is* this?"

"I said, do you love M?"

"No, I don't love M." She frowns.

Mina and Minho's eyes light up with curiosity.

"If you don't love him then why do you hang out with him?"

"It was only a few times."

Now the voice comes fast and low-pitched. "So, you don't love me—for real?" It's M calling.

"No, I don't." Moving the phone away from her ear, she responds mechanically: "Yeah...yeah...yeah...so...yeah...so, do *you* love *me*?"

9

"What? Of course I do. Didn't you know?"

"No I didn't."

"Why not?"

"I don't know."

"How couldn't you know?"

"I don't know why I don't know."

Crystal sneaks a glance at Minho. He's grabbed the remote, turned on the TV, and is switching to a new channel every three seconds. A giraffe drinks from a water hole, legs spread and long neck bent way over.

"That's weird."

Crystal remains silent.

"Really weird."

"What's weird?"

M starts to say something then stops. He tries again, then falls silent once more, then he ends the call, his voice listless. Crystal feels empty and has a raging thirst. The curiosity in Mina and Minho's eyes is bright. Crystal looks blankly at each of them in turn and heads for the kitchen.

"What was that all about?"

"Who was that?"

"What's going on? Who was it?" says Mina again as she follows Crystal into the kitchen. "Come on—tell me."

"I need some water."

Mina fills a coffee mug with water and offers it to her.

"It was M. I'm done with him." There's no trace of emotion on Crystal's face but her voice suddenly rises in a lovely, silky tone. "Mind if I smoke?"

"No way!" Mina and Minho cry out at the same time.

Crystal smiles peevishly.

"Good job, girl," says Mina. "After the midterms I'll set you up with someone."

"Thanks!" gushes Crystal as she falls into Mina's arms.

"Hey…," says Mina.

"What?"

"What about Minho?"

"Yeah?" Crystal grins at Mina. "Really? You're serious? Sure…why not?"

"Gotcha!" Mina and Minho cry out together.

"Hey, lay off, Mina." Crystal gives Minho a wave. "Relax—*Oppa*'s cool, he can handle it."

"Don't get carried away!"

Again Crystal falls into Mina's arms. "You see…"

"What?"

"I love you."

"Then you're definitely crazy. Hey, Minho."

"Yeah?"

"Time for cram school."

Minho's cellphone rings. He goes to his room and closes the door. It has to be his girlfriend, thinks Crystal. She eases up to the door and tries to catch some of the conversation but all she can make out are fleeting words, exclamations, giggles. With a long face she returns to the living room, just before Minho emerges from his room. Crystal regards him. Minho goes over to Mina and gives her a light kick on the leg.

"Get up, sow," Minho says, giving her a wide grin.

"If I'm a sow then you're a fat-ass."

"I'm out of here." Minho slings his backpack over his shoulder and heads for the door.

"Where're you going?" Mina shouts.

"Yeah, where?" says Crystal.

Without answering, Minho opens the door.

"Hey, fat-ass. You're meeting Yujin, I know it! I'm going to tell Mom you skipped cram school to see your little sweetie."

"Yujin *ŏnni*, to you. And I'm not skipping school. Mind your own business, little girl."

"Beat it, Minho."

"Have fun, Crystal, see you later!"

The door closes on Crystal giving a belated wave.

Outside, evening lights are brightening the city. A blood-red afterglow has quickly settled on the living room. It's the time of day when patches of high clouds layered with soft pastel colors emerge, when buildings and broadleaf trees reach out with long fingers of shadow.

Crystal and Mina, as they've done countless times before, pack their backpacks, tidy the living room, fix their hair and straighten their clothing, and make their leisurely way outside. The three-note warble echoes in the hallway as the door locks. Crystal pushes the elevator button. Mina looks up at the ceiling, mumbling like an old woman, then sighs. After a few gentle openings and closings the elevator deposits them at ground level. Outside, the afterglow drapes the ground and dusk slowly sweeps up the remaining daylight. A silver car zips by. Their heads turn, following it. When it disappears Crystal locks her right arm in Mina's left arm. And then they too are no longer visible, lost among the cherry blossoms.

Crystal studies the thesis statement handed out by the instructor. She needs to supply a supporting detail—what's it going to be? But then she's sidetracked remembering the phone call from M. What was he trying to tell her? She scratches her thigh, a concentration tactic—*get back on topic!*—but it doesn't work. M said he loves her. Crystal realizes the declaration angered her and now she feels that same anger rising. She thinks she's too young to love anyone. Even when she's older, better to steer clear of something so impractical. *It's tacky. It's useless.*

Do I have to fall in love? Just give me some romance comics—they have everything I need to know about loving someone…to hell with all that. Back comes the anger. She jerks her head up in agitation. Finds herself eye to eye with the instructor. With a smile he approaches. Crystal doesn't break contact with his slate-gray eyes. She takes the handout, puts on a serious face, and asks a series of trivial questions about it. Then she says:

"Your eyes look kind of blue today."

"You think so?" Wide-eyed, the instructor gives a mischievous grin.

She nods.

"I wonder why," he says in English.

But the truth is, it's all Crystal's fault. All the boys she's gone out with so far are like nice little spotted calves. The moment she sees these nice little calves she inevitably wants to hang out with them. But there's a problem: once she starts dating them she expects them to have the maturity and stability of married men in their mid-thirties and not the innocent charm of nice little calves. M doesn't know what to do with himself and Crystal gets frustrated. And so today, once again, her love life has been stamped with the type of frustration that the weekend soap operas are riddled with. But because her spotted calves are well aware of their own cluelessness, in her presence they don't try to pretty up their childish feelings of inferiority or their immature rants about society. They're fine with their own cluelessness, and they prize their relationship with her—they don't abuse her, don't demand nude pictures of her in disgusting pornographic poses. Going out with them is like a weekend of playing house on a farm—getting up early, putting on a lacy apron, digging the radishes, gathering the eggs, and milking the cow. Sure, all students need a change of pace—their lives are destructive and barren.

What they need is rest. So where does *loving* someone fit in? The clueless calves get infected with romanticism. Spring fever—how else can you explain it?

But the truth is, Crystal is the dumb one. Not because she's immature but because she goes to a cram school. The private education system in P City looks down upon P City's broken public education system, offering a customized and quality education based on a student's achievement level. It's not a solution, merely a gigantic market that feeds off the broken public school system. The cram schools make a place for themselves by seizing on the flaws and weaknesses of the public schools, creating a massive market, and so they succeed, but that's it. They analyze everything from a business's point of view. They try to provide the best service to their consumers, but they lack any kind of spirit. And what is spirit anyway? How much of a demand is there for it? And how does one market spirit? When one cram-school guru comes up with a document full of English in response to these questions, another guru counters with a document full of Chinese characters. They compare notes, nod in agreement, and adjourn to their whiskey bar, where they straighten their ties and button their cuffs and exchange tips about other places to drink that they've discovered. Their lists of "must-read books" include the game-changing classics of Western civilization. The instructors then flash these crammed lists and tell their students, "If you want to get into an Ivy League school or even P University, you need to read this stuff, there's no other way." The kids nod, fold the list in half, and tuck it in their backpack. Done—nothing further to think about or concern themselves with. *The day is short and there are loads of other students like me. Do I feel lonely? No way—I'm not the only one.* There goes a student. And another student. They meet at an intersection, shake hands, smile, and go their separate ways.

High school takes students down one of three paths: one for the really smart kids, who already know the steps they have to take to maintain their elite standing and better avail themselves of the opportunities afforded them; one for most kids, whose only option is to endure in the hope that university has to be better than this; and stuck in between these two are the students who have lost their way, who engage in useless fantasies, who suffer from depression and end up killing themselves. The kids who commit suicide do so not because of the suffering they've experienced but because they know nothing about life and think of suicide as a fantasy or delude themselves into thinking death would be an answer for their suffering. Crystal, needless to say, is one of the really smart kids. She's a model child who humbly accepts that which she's ignorant of and bows to the knowledge of grown-ups— or at least she pretends to. She never really learns anything. To camouflage her lack of learning she processes the grown-ups' instructions verbatim and is quick to adapt and mimic. The grown-ups are scared of a girl like her. *You're smart all right,* they might want to tell her, *but you're still only a kid, a child, all show and no go, you've got a long way to go till you're fully formed. You need to learn about the world or else.... Doesn't it scare you? The future is unknown: it's dark; it's cold, hard reality and green stacks of money; it's orbiting out there somewhere, and who knows when and where it will land. Look at my wrinkled face, that's what comes from life in the open—the air, the sunshine, the humiliation and frustration, they've ruined me.*

And Crystal might respond: *The last thing I'll do is live your shitty life.*

Clutching her pen, she moves on to the next supporting detail.

Grown-ups like to use words they don't understand. And that planet you're talking about, you've never set foot on it.

Just another adamant denial of the bullshit of grown-ups before it's on to the next detail. Crystal is confident about her future. Confident because none of this stuff is her fault, because it was all fabricated before her arrival. She arrived after everything was in place; she wasn't born until everything was already prepared. Accordingly, if she can have everything, it's probably because she arrived at the perfect time and place with everything awaiting her. The universe has *chosen* her and she welcomes being chosen. Since her world existed before her arrival, just like her language had its set grammar and tone, all that remains for her is passive learning. But Crystal is not about to complain: even if she yearns to make herself unique, she's bound and determined to choke back such urges and submit to the establishment. She is perfect because she is unfeeling and doesn't know love, and she is untainted because she was never on her own as she grew up. And now here she is looking at a chalkboard. She sees a perfect world of sleek numbers and lines, and a door to this world that's wide open. But she's already here. She forgets about M. The world dazzles her. The instructor knocks on his desk—time's up. Crystal looks at her assignment. Perfect!

DEATH

The bus stops and the waiting kids pile on. Crystal and Mina have barely crawled on, grabbed strap handles, before the bus pulls away, rocking and swaying. It's full to bursting, but quiet—so quiet they can hear what sounds like someone crying. The sound grows and the passengers' eyes shift to the rear. Three girls in green school uniforms are crying, their faces glistening with tears—Pak Chiye, a student at P School, killed herself the night before.

She jumped from the roof of the five-story building where students rent cubicles. She and Mina had palled around since kindergarten and had lived in the same neighborhood until three years ago, when Mina's family moved to their luxury condominium near Crystal's apartment complex. Just before taking her life, Chiye texted Mina saying she wanted to kill herself. Mina hadn't seen her lately and wasn't sure whether to take her seriously—maybe it was just a sudden whim? Either way Mina was glad she had texted—the first message from Chiye in a long while—and she had been about to reply when her cellphone died. As soon as she got home from cram school she charged the battery and texted Chiye back, but no reply. In the meantime, Chiye had told her mother she was off to her cubicle to spend the night preparing for exams and that she'd go straight to school the following morning. The other students in the building reported nothing out of the ordinary; she didn't look or act troubled. She studied till one in the morning then went up to the roof and jumped. There was no note, no instructions for disposing of her belongings. Left behind on her desk were her Ethics and Morals study guide, a pencil, a black Magic Marker, a notepad, an old math test she'd crumpled and then uncrumpled, and a half-eaten container of plain yogurt.

Crystal and Mina don't interact for the rest of the way to school. After they've arrived Crystal keeps glancing at Mina, trying to read her. On the whole Mina seems fine, except at the school gate she momentarily loses her balance. Once in the classroom she collapses into her seat. Other girls gather around her. Crystal hovers uncertainly on the periphery before returning to her seat. Mina doesn't cry or shout; she merely looks a bit tired and hungry. With an effort she sits up, scratches her elbow, passes a hand through her hair, takes her pencil, and flips through her stupid workbook. When Crystal texts her, "Buck up," Mina takes her phone from her pocket, silences it, and stuffs it into her bag. Crystal is flustered. From the PA in the classroom comes the head teacher's voice announcing it's the last day of testing and encouraging the students to keep up the good work and finish strong. But the news of Chiye's suicide has sent a shock wave through the kids and they've forgotten the test momentarily while they attempt to retrieve their views on life and death, which are more or less uniform but contain a few variations. These views they're considering are kept in a dusty black container that's larger than it should be. The kids tilt their containers this way and that, tap on it, sniff at the contents, wipe off the dust, then try to find a box that's a better fit for the time being. But before returning their views to the original container they gather in the classroom then sweep into the hallway to tromp around as if possessed: like the boy who cried wolf as he chased off dark clouds with his herder's staff. Then the darkness disappears from their expressions as fast as it gathered and their faces are placid again, as if nothing has happened. The bell for first period sounds and the exam is passed out. The kids nudge their black boxes aside with their feet, take pens in hands, and soon all eyes are fixed on the exam. All except Mina's. She alone continues to gaze skyward, tapping her shepherd's staff.

Crystal is caught in a dilemma: What look should she adopt; what expression should she wear? She looks around. Everyone's manner appears perfectly appropriate. They may not have known her well, this student from the school close by who resembled them in many ways, but now that they've heard the news of her suicide they seem to know how to respond. *Am I the only one, the one person who's without a clue?* She feels uneasy. Should she make herself look tired? Put her head on her desk and close her eyes? Lament to the sky? She just doesn't know. Outside, the sun is playing peekaboo behind lazy clouds—a peaceful scene. Can she just sit and watch it? Or maybe she shouldn't?

Crystal knew Chiye, but only through Mina. She offered a bright hello to Chiye when she and Mina ran into her, but if Mina wasn't there she'd simply pass by, though it was awkward. Chiye was too distant for Crystal to show interest in, yet too close to neglect. Back when Mina transferred here and was looking uncertainly around her new classroom, when she began to get close to Crystal but still was closer to Chiye, she used to yak incessantly about her. There was the day she and Chiye graduated from kindergarten, and then their first day of grade school, and then the day Chiye turned nine, and then an adventure with Chiye in the caves at the DMZ. Mina's reminiscing reached its apex when she talked about the year she and Chiye took a trip to Kyoto with Minho—Chiye eating sushi, Chiye eating *tonkatsu donburi*, Chiye eating *unagi donburi*, Chiye getting sick on *unagi donburi*, Chiye taking an antacid that made her drowsy, Chiye falling asleep, Chiye waking up and yawning, Chiye taking photos, Chiye being photographed, Chiye dropping her ice cream on the floor, Chiye picking it up and eating it—all with Mina, of course—and with Minho taking pictures of the two of them. Back then Crystal had doubts about Mina's relationship with Chiye—were they friends or were they lovers? For Crystal, Mina had been a big question mark. But at the start of the new semester Mina quickly cut back on her stories about Chiye. There were no new stories about her or adventures involving her—they now went to different schools, their homes were farther apart, and Mina, shocked at the study fever at this new school, signed up for Crystal's cram school. Which meant four hours of supplementary classes every night. It was hard for Mina to keep up with. In time she no longer lined up a train of anecdotes about Chiye, once delivered in a bubbly voice. But still Crystal wondered: What was there about Chiye that had gotten Mina so psyched? Would Mina now get psyched over *her*? And now that Chiye was gone, Crystal wonders even more. But she can't very well ask Mina that—how could she?

I don't think it's my problem that Chiye bombed an exam and killed herself. I don't know why she did it, and I don't want to know when I honestly don't even know where she lived.

Satisfied with this conclusion, her thoughts now clear in

her mind, Crystal scans the notes she's been reviewing for the exam, but then takes one last glance at Mina. And with that glance she finds the epitome of a schoolgirl who's just learned of her friend's suicide. A girl emanating the beauty of an elegant math formula. Crystal wants to open her notebook and come to grips with that formula. The formula is magnificent, its beauty overpowering, leaving her breathless. She imagines, shining six inches behind Mina's head, a three-layered aura set in Bohemian stained glass. Glittering gold wheels, large and elaborate, turn busily but without a sound. Even that ray of sunlight falling across her gently lowered ivory-colored forehead, is as precise as an atomic clock. How can something that comes from the heart look so perfect? Crystal is dubious. Mina looks unbelievably perfect, as if she had polished this façade for the very moment Chiye threw herself from the rooftop. Overwhelmed by Mina's flawless beauty, Crystal manages to collect herself and wonders: How vexed would Mina be if Chiye hadn't killed herself? Gone would be the opportunity for Mina to display her perfected performance, gone the opportunity for Crystal to appreciate her rare beauty. Then is this a good thing, something to be thankful for, a reason to love Mina more? *No, it's not.* Crystal feels Mina's exceptional flair stab at her heart, choking her up. *I want it.* More than ever she longs for that flair. *I want it. I want it. I want it.* The sentence repeats in her mind, that and nothing else. But this objective is unattainable, and it turns into rage. Glaring spitefully at her, she feels Mina's sorrow magnify inside her, a sadness so close and yet out of reach. She is jealous of Mina's sorrow, no longer of Mina's friend Chiye. She stares desperately at her exam and finds a realm of silence and peace, perfect and eternal. Suddenly she feels an outpouring of love toward the exam. Wanting to crush Mina, she turns to the first page. And to the next page, and the one after that, peace reigning throughout. Crystal understands everything written on the test, the question she's now focusing on and the ones before it and after it. She is at peace in this world in which she has perfect control of everything. While she tackles the exam questions, Mina recedes into the distance. Crystal longs for her to go, keep going, and never return.

Mina turned in blank answer sheets for all three of her midterm exams, earning herself a summons to the school office. It was a perfect climax and ending: Mina the *femme tragique*. What can Crystal say for herself? She feels like a complete failure. Looking out the window and watching the clouds drift past, she smokes one cigarette after another but can't allay her concern. Instead she sprays air freshener and cranks the window wide open. She changes into a black skirt and red stockings and then, while sneezing three times in a row, manages to stuff her graded midterms into her handbag along with her credit card and cellphone. After checking her watch she fixes her hair in the mirror. From her door to the elevator to the playground in the apartment complex she keeps trying to reach Mina, but Mina's not answering. Crystal flags down a taxi. When she tells the driver her destination—the posh high-rise where Mina lives with her family—his expression eases.

She finds Mina sprawled out in the hallway outside her apartment, looking up at the light in the ceiling. "Hey, Mina." She circles her—*what now?*—then grabs her leg and pulls, bringing a spluttered exclamation from Mina. Crystal lets go of her leg and laughs. Mina manages to scowl and smile at the same time. They're both smiling. Slowly Mina covers her face with her hands. A faint moan escapes through her fingers, sounding indignant more than sorrowful, like a door creaking open, a live toad being lowered into a pot of boiling oil, a person who has forever lost any memory of her home or its address, a curse that continues till the moment she dies. How could such a sound come from Mina's mouth? As Mina caves in to the extremity of her emotions Crystal can think of no way to help other than joining her friend in looking up at the ceiling, her arms folded.

Finally, Mina removes her hands from her face: "Let's go."

Crystal and Pyŏl are clinging to each other as they sing. Bathed in the rotating colors of the disco light, Pyŏl paws at Crystal's chest. Mina chugs a can of beer. Chŏng'u seems to be getting a charge out of watching her: whenever she plunks an empty can onto the table he grins and hands her a new one from a plastic bag. Mina plunks down an empty can, he hands her another. Down goes another empty can, out comes a full one. Crystal pushes Pyŏl away and shakes a fist at Chŏng'u.

"Stop it, she's had enough!"

"Hey, I want mooore," Mina slurs. "Gonna have mooore…up yours."

Chŏng'u looks in the bag. "Only one left."

Pyŏl starts a new song and pulls Crystal to him. As they start kissing again, Chŏng'u forgets about the beer, flips through the songbook, then gets up saying he's going out for cigarettes.

Crystal frees her mouth from Pyŏl's long enough to call Chŏng'u over and hand him money. "Get me a pack too, please? And something to sober her up." The moment he's out the door she and Pyŏl glue themselves back together. The microphone drops to the floor. Mina drops to the floor. A new song starts and ends, the performance rating comes up on the screen followed by canned applause, and then there's another song. Crystal and Pyŏl are on the sofa, licking and groping each other. Just as they're about to stick their hands in each other's pants Chŏng'u returns.

They reluctantly untangle themselves. Chŏng'u watches, exasperated, as Pyŏl buttons Crystal's blouse and she straightens his tie. Pyŏl walks out, a cigarette projecting from his mouth. Crystal takes Mina's hand as she lies listless on the floor, wraps it around the bottle of tonic Chŏng'u brought, and rubs her shoulder. Mina doesn't respond. Chŏng'u pushes a number on the selector and sings along with the new song. Crystal opens Mina's mouth and closes it. Her jaws hinge mechanically. "She's not breathing," she says to Chŏng'u. Lost in the song, he doesn't hear her. "Hey! She's not breathing!" she yells. He slowly turns toward her. "She's not breathing!" she yells again. He approaches, bewildered, and together they shake her. Still no response. Chŏng'u flips Mina over and raps her sharply three times on the back.

"Is that supposed to get her breathing?" says Crystal.

Chŏng'u doesn't reply; this is *serious*. Crystal tries to straighten Mina's disheveled hair. Silently, Chŏng'u continues his peculiar attempt at first aid while Crystal helplessly drinks the tonic. Finally Chŏng'u flips Mina back over and attempts CPR.

"Stop! No more!" Crystal screams, drawing a look from him. "What's your name anyway?"

"Chŏng'u. We better call 911."

"You're sure she's not breathing?"

"Yeah."

Crystal likes it that he's so cool and reserved.

Pyŏl comes back. "The fuck?"

Crystal and Chŏng'u don't answer, merely regard Mina. Pyŏl comes over to Mina and calls her name. No response. Crystal punches in *911* on her cellphone. The room they're in looks shabby in the bright light that has replaced the dim, rotating party light. Just as Crystal hits Talk on her cellphone Mina grabs her thigh. "Hey…I'm okay."

"You are?"

"But it's hard to breathe."

"She's breathing," Crystal announces.

"Yeah?"

"Fuck, she scared the hell out of me!"

"Hey, Pyŏl, stop swearing," Crystal barks.

"Fuck."

"Fuck? Did you say *fuck*? You did say *fuck* again, didn't you."

Crystal lunges at him, starts beating him. He doesn't resist, just accepts the kicks and punches. Chŏng'u flinches, then returns to his songbook and picks out a new tune.

"I said I'm having a hard time breathing!" Mina's voice is lost as the song begins, and then Chŏng'u is singing—a hit with a fast tempo. Chŏng'u wails away. Crystal helps Mina sit up. Mina's eyes are red and teary.

"Hey, Mina? You okay?"

"My head hurts."

"Why?"

"It just does. I'm fucking depressed. I want to kill myself."

"Why do you say that?" Crystal examines her. Mina has a pained expression, but Crystal feels numb—and frustrated by her numbness. Crystal brings her face closer to Mina's an inch at a time. At close range she can magnify Mina's lips, eyes, nose, and the streaks from dried tears on her cheeks. But no matter how close she gets, she can't grasp her own emotions in these details. To disguise the void of her feelings Crystal crinkles her face theatrically.

Tears ooze out through Mina's closed eyelids. "I wanna go home. I wanna kill myself. My head hurts super bad. I can't breathe. Feel like I'm suffocating. It's so…so…stupid, this place."

"Mina, stop it."

"What's the matter?" Mina opens her eyes.

"You're scaring me."

"Really?"

Mina sees Crystal move her lips. The colored lights rotate again. Chŏng'u wails. Mina can't hear Crystal. She can't hear a thing. "Hey. I can't hear you. Say it again. Tell me why—why do I scare you?"

Crystal moves her lips again. The lights briefly flicker. Before them are six television screens and on each of them the same girl wearing the same smile performs the same dance, and the same song lyrics run across the screens, a line at a time.

Mina, ashen-faced, pushes Crystal, gets up, and grabs the doorknob. It doesn't turn. Crystal takes Mina by the arm, her lips moving. Mina can't hear her. She tenses with fear and with a great effort tries the knob again. It won't move. Crystal grabs both her arms and shakes her.

"Let go." The words barely escape Mina's lips.

Crystal is flustered—Mina *never* talks like that. "Mina, what are you *doing*? That's the wrong way. The door's over *here*."

Mina startles and lets go of what she's holding—the handle on a milky pink plastic vase containing an artificial petunia. Pyŏl and Chŏng'u watch Mina, baffled. Mina doesn't understand what's happening to her. Her only thought is that they're all making fun of her. And then she registers their confused expressions. And she looks at the vase with the petunia and thinks she realizes what they're up to—they got her dead drunk until she passed out, then wrapped her hand around the handle of the vase. But considering the shape she's in—tongue not working, drunk and scared out of her mind—she'll never get them to own up to it. All she can do is slump to the floor, bawling like a toddler. Crystal grabs a microphone and sings. It's a slow, quiet love song. She caresses Mina's shoulder as she sings. Mina's crying dies down. Pyŏl goes out the door. During the intro to the next song Crystal bends down to Mina. "You okay? Aren't you thirsty? How about a bottle of water?"

Mina shakes her head.

Pyŏl comes back with a Baskin-Robbins ice cream cone and hands it to Mina. With a piercing stare at the cone Mina says, "Of all the thirty-one flavors this is the one I like the least." Crystal and Chŏng'u glare at Pyŏl—*nice try!* Mina tries to get up but slumps back to the floor, the impact causing her to drop the cone. She bursts into tears. The others look frightened. In no time the ice cream melts. Chŏng'u pops open the last can of beer. Crystal and Pyŏl light cigarettes for each other. Mina's crying grows louder. Crystal presses a random button on the song selector and hits Start. Out comes a popular song from the 1970s about a couple lying in the grass. Chŏng'u giggles at the lyrics that pass across the screens and manages to spill his beer. Mina vomits on the floor.

The four of them climb the narrow stairs from the basement karaoke place. Outside it's dark and a mishmash of pop songs fight for attention like yowling cats. With Mina in tow Crystal is about to blend into the crowd on the busy street when Pyŏl grabs her shoulder. "Bye." She gives him a cute grin. "Take care." She watches Pyŏl and Chŏng'u—lingering where they parted—grow small as she and Mina walk away. The two boys have their arms around each other's shoulders and are smiling idiotic smiles. Crystal gives Pyŏl a loving look as he recedes into the distance. Still wearing that warm expression, she turns to Mina without really thinking about it and the next moment the world turns black. She realizes she's all alone with Mina. Mina's arm on her shoulder oozes cold sweat. Crystal's smile disappears. They turn down a street lit only by yellow sodium lights, altogether different from the busy street. Crystal lets out a faint sigh. Mina lights a cigarette and draws the attention of a middle-aged man fanning himself in front of a grocery store; he looks like he wants to brain her with a brick. Crystal leads Mina. Mina gapes up at the dark sky crisscrossed by a mesh of power lines.

"Chiye's gone," Mina says. After a long pause she continues, as if ashamed of herself, "What do I do now?" She sounds stiff and awkward, as if reading from a book.

Tense, Crystal watches her. She doesn't like it when Mina looks pained like this; she hates it. She doesn't want to talk, not about something so grim, no matter whom she's with. She wonders, of course, what exactly Mina feels. But if Mina is about to *tell* her how she feels…now that's scary, Crystal doesn't like that. Damn the contradictions she feels! Her rationality demands that she block the flow of her emotions toward Mina. It's easier said than done. Crystal is unable to refuse the demands of those emotions, they're so massive, so powerful, so forceful yet dark. Is it love she feels, or jealousy? Whatever it is, it's new, complex, and frightening, and it leaves her feeling as stiff as a log—who needs all that? She's afraid. She feels inky water lapping at her ankles and she's afraid of what lies beneath. Gingerly she lifts a foot from the black, lukewarm liquid, and at that moment her eyes meet Mina's. And in those eyes she reads: *How could you?* How could she what? What huge mistake involving Mina is she guilty of? Nothing comes to mind. Then why does Mina have that look in her eyes? Crystal is troubled. She feels she's been dropped into a city where everyone speaks a different language. Familiar things no longer feel familiar. She wants to escape this ambiguity that so upsets her, that's so unusual to her. She has to find a place with clarity. She pulls her other foot out of the murky water and says: "Mina, I'm sleepy. I want to go home."

Mina's face blanches. She's barely able to collect herself. Crystal doesn't notice. Mina nods and tosses her cigarette into the street. Their eyes meet but their lips don't move. Mina crumples her empty cigarette pack and tosses it as far as she can. And then they are moving in different directions, without saying goodbye. Only the moon is left and it too is filtered by the clouds.

MINA

The classroom is a cacophony of hellos, high fives, screams, bursts of laughter, curses, chairs tumbling, the door opening and quickly slamming shut. The class monitor's announcement of a birthday party for the homeroom teacher generates even more of a buzz.

The bell for the start of class rings and the students stifle all noise, waiting for the arrival of their teacher. The door opens, firecrackers go off, and the students shoot up and launch into "Happy Birthday"—or is it "Benevolent Teacher" that's supposed to come first? The confusion makes for an awkward dissonance, and when the teacher bursts into delighted laughter mayhem reigns. With her eyes shut, Crystal daydreams that there's a huge cheesecake waiting for her in the refrigerator at home—or maybe that Mina will bring one when she comes over. She hears chairs scraping against the floor. She opens her eyes to see most of her classmates back in their seats with beaming smiles as they feast on cookies, fruit, and soft drinks, their teacher gathering her gifts in a shopping bag, the monitor cutting the cake. Crystal remains sitting. A grinning boy is coming in her direction, a dud firecracker in his hand. She looks down, staring at her textbook.

He passes her on the way to his locker. Glancing at Mina's unoccupied seat, Crystal reaches into her pocket for her cellphone. Mina's been absent for two days: either her phone's off or she's just not returning calls. Crystal tries Mina's number, hangs up when there's no answer, then tries her number in vain one more time.

"Mina's absent again," she says aloud, and everyone turns to face her. The impression she gives is that without Mina something is missing. Staring blankly out the window and scratching her thigh, she gets up and heads for the door. Along the way she loses her balance for a moment and lists to the side and in the next moment she bumps her head against the wall. Shaken by the stares of her classmates, she staggers to the door and out into the hallway. The sky wears its perpetual film of yellow dust but the air is weighted with moisture—a heavy rain is on the way. Groups of students in blue tracksuits pass her in the hallway trailing a sweaty odor. She bumps into them as she wanders aimlessly from one end of the hall to the other.

"Hey, are you okay? You look tired."

She feels a tug on her arm, startles, and looks up to see Chiwŏn's face, perpetually pale and weary, right in front of her. She looks concerned.

"I guess I had too much to drink last night."

"How did you do on the midterms?"

"Get lost, Chiwŏn!" Making her off-balance way back to the classroom, she sits, puts her headphones back on, and replays the song she was listening to on her MP3 player, "How to Disappear Completely" by Radiohead. And she thinks about Mina who has disappeared.

For no particular reason Mina often cuts off contact with everybody and misses school. Which means she's never earned a perfect attendance award—but she couldn't care less. Nor do her parents consider attendance all that important as long as she goes to school often enough, studies hard enough, gets good enough grades, and is thought well enough of by her peers and teachers. She does enough to avoid requiring much in the way of parental attention. She's never crossed a bridge from which she couldn't return, and her personality hasn't been warped by despair. She is growing up with a good education and the well-balanced sensibility characteristic of the children of parents who grew up with a good education; she has lived her life free and easy and has never crossed the line. Crystal envies this girl more than she would like to admit, Mina who Crystal thinks possesses a free spirit that's inconsistent with society in these times. How can she do that? Sometimes Crystal is tormented by this question. Compared with Mina's liberated, beautiful, and adequately abundant life, Crystal feels her own is insubstantial and unhealthy, like mass-produced doughnuts dripping with trans fats. Mina is relaxed and fearless and, as far as Crystal can tell, she's never been hurt. *How is it possible?*

Mina has several peculiar pastimes, one of which is that she periodically goes into a closet and doesn't come out till her MP3 player's battery dies. *It's so comfortable in there,* she'd say. *Really?* To test Mina's thesis Crystal tried it herself, with her own MP3 player. She found Mina's closet boring, dark, and dead. The stillness was frightening, and it was too dark to see anything. The music was too loud and sharp. In the close, suffocating darkness she could feel the visceral ugliness of the human body. Her legs and arms, unable to stretch out, were useless appendages of skin and bone. She went on the prowl but felt nothing except for last winter's clothing, smelled nothing but the heavy scent of lavender air freshener. She exited the closet hating Mina and disappointed in herself.

Another of Mina's proclivities, a rather extravagant one, is to lie about having lost her MP3 player. That way she could buy a new one to add to her diverse collection. As soon as she hears a new player is on the market, she loses her current one. By now her "lost" MP3 players have filled a wooden box in a back corner of the closet—five iPods, two each of iRivers and Samsungs, a Sharp, and a Sony. The two Samsungs are the same model and color, one of which she deluded herself into actually thinking she really lost. She can't explain how this particular interest developed.

"When I reach a hundred I'll show my mom," Mina tells Crystal when she's drunk. "For revenge."

"Revenge for what?"

But Mina doesn't answer.

When Minho learned about Mina's luxurious pastime he snatched her new sixty-four gigabyte iPod and hit her with it. Mina pulled down the collar of her blouse so Crystal could see the small but deep gash a corner of the iPod made in her neck. "And here…" she showed Crystal dark purple swelling and a scab on her left shoulder. Crystal tried in vain to imagine dependable, well-mannered Minho attacking Mina with an iPod.

"What did your mom say?"

"She doesn't know."

"Why not?"

"Well, I told the idiot I'd kill myself if he ever squeals on me."

"And he believes you."

"Of course."

"How can you be sure?"

"I went on a hunger strike."

Her three-day hunger strike brought a formal apology from Minho and a new iPod from her mother once Mina showed her the broken one. Since then Minho hasn't interfered with Mina's desires.

When people talk about a rich kid with a good education, they often testify to her innocence—*she's not aware of how privileged she is; you won't find her bragging or showing off; she's even humble!* This kind of assessment brings to mind a poor kid who is so perfectly naïve that she doesn't even realize how poor she is. The clear difference between the two is: if the poor kid's ignorance of her poverty is a sin only to herself, the rich kid's ignorance of her affluence is a sin against others. Take an innocent kid who crushes an earthworm with her foot for fun. Clearly that's bad. But her parents don't dwell on it. Instead they encourage their kid, they praise her, and if you were to challenge them they'd say, *Well, what do you expect, she's only a kid, she's got a lot to learn.* To maintain their control, parents inevitably downplay their own sins; they tell their kids the world has only two kinds of people: those who do things and those who get things done to them, there's no one in between. *The life we were never allowed is the life you'll have, there's no other option. It's a fair fight*, the parents insist, *the results are transparent. So swallow your pride, accept defeat, and do things our way from now on.* The problem is, the concept of a fair fight is a perversion of reality. The world keeps slowly turning with one part of the city maintaining a closed and exclusive middle-class lifestyle that is selfish, ignorant, and irresponsible, all of its practitioners keeping quiet about how that lifestyle came to be and how it manages to repeat itself— how sinful it is—while in another section of the city the lives of the losers slowly sink beneath all the pressures and sins of the winners, though no one calls for accountability. Where is it going, this world—to what end? No one knows. It's an unnavigable marsh, and it's on this footing of ignorance and sin that Mina's virtues have accumulated. But is anyone about to corner her for her sins, blame her for her ignorance? Such a possibility has long since gone extinct in P City. To the world at large Mina's father is a translator and fiction writer. But he hasn't translated a book in six months, and his creative writing career consists of one story collection published five years ago by a prestigious press; it earned a single review in an influential daily's weekend edition, struggled to sell out its first press run, then disappeared from readers' memories. How then does Mina's family get along? Until Mina's father won the lottery they depended entirely on her mother's earnings. Their lifestyle was typical of an educated family that had placed their future on the mother's shoulders. But this was before Crystal met Mina, three years ago, when Mina and her family moved to their current apartment near Crystal's when Mina's father won the lottery. The cost of their new luxury apartment was almost as much as the jackpot from the lottery, but they paid only half in cash and the rest with a loan. They celebrated with a ski trip to the Czech Republic. Upon returning they filled their new home with fancy furniture and appliances. The quarterly assessments show the apartment appreciating in value slowly but steadily, a secure and worry-free asset. They live off a home equity loan taken out against the apartment, and with the help of a realtor who's a distant relative, Mina's father managed to purchase an apartment in a neighboring city that draws a lot of investors. Three months later they sold it for a thirty-five percent profit. With those proceeds and the remainder of the lottery money they invested in a diversified real-estate fund that proved successful. Six months ago Mina's father left for Pusan vowing to write a masterpiece.

When the news of Mina's father's jackpot-aided purchase of a swank apartment in a middle-class sector of the city reached his network of friends, former classmates, and colleagues—most of them impoverished intellectuals—none of them criticized or scorned him. No one was upset by his metamorphosis. *Of course, the lottery—you pay your money and you take your chances,* thought an ascetic friend, who with his ascetic smile soon forgot the matter. Most of the time he kept his ascetic brain half empty, as an ascetic should. Mina's father's humble friends returned from the housewarming party and reported to their impecunious wives, who nodded ceaselessly, marveling at the family's practical and excellent choice. His colleagues, however, didn't hide their envy. Booze-pickled, reeking of tobacco, they tended to forego deconstructing and reconstructing theoretical foreign texts and fantasizing about the world in favor of agonizing over how to immerse themselves in the polluted air of P City and peddle knowledge in the private education market.

Crystal detested, really detested, private tutors, but acknowledged their capability. Mina, through her father's connections, got top-shelf tutors at reasonable rates. He always seemed to have a passel of them on hand, and Mina selected wisely from among them, squeezing in drawing, ballet, even traditional Indian yoga and vegan diet classes. For a while she seriously thought about home schooling or an alternative school for her secondary education. But eventually she chose a public school, and except for an occasional get-together for authentic Thai food with the kids from her drawing class— the children of her father's friends—she devoted herself to cram school and private tutoring.

Seeing Mina in this light, Crystal occasionally flew into an inexplicable rage. The Mina she saw then was an uppity kid so spoiled and engrossed in Spider Solitaire that a table full of brain-zappingly sugary royal French dessert cakes drew not a glance from her. Of course, Crystal could also eat as many royal French dessert cakes as she wanted. Money wasn't an issue. In fact, Crystal was more likely to see cash or a check on the family dining table than cakes—which were of no interest to her parents. They were happier going out for free-range duck stew on the weekends or watching the latest blockbuster movie to hit ten million at the box office.

Such preferences were definitely not a matter of money. For instance, Paek Hanch'ŏl, a colleague of Mina's father—a translator-poet-photographer-essayist-illustrator—and his family were not particularly well off but pursued the table-full-of-royal-French-dessert-cakes lifestyle. Pinched for money, they still managed to conceal their class by playing let's-pretend and loading up on expensive cakes, which they put on display for all to see. The cakes, of course, were as sweet as an angel's wing and you'd be in heaven as they melted on the tip of your tongue, but apart from such minutiae the family had nothing to show for themselves. They bought their jackets (stuffed with chicken down!) at a street market, couldn't afford cellphones, couldn't afford private English lessons for the kids, worried about the monthly payment for the air conditioner, used a six-year-old desktop-sized laptop, and rented an apartment in an outdated building on the margins of the city. What's so great about that? In the luxury apartment that Mina's family occupies, the living room floor is made of marble and Chinese juniper wood, and is overlain with a Moroccan area rug. Does the Paek family criticize or envy them? Not at all; they seem unconcerned. They appear to be people without ambition. What kind of life is *that*? You could whisk them off, deposit them in a coffin, nail it shut, and stuff it in a grave, and they would gladly accept their fate, smile nice smiles, and close their eyes. That's not goodness at work, it's a lack of intelligence. They don't scorn Mina's mother's collection of luxury European handbags, they don't buy lottery tickets, they don't send their little girl to an English-language kindergarten, and they don't speak proudly—sparkles in their eyes—of their humble life. *A poor family with no plan? That's messed up! Their fancy cakes are too precious to eat, they rot and end up ruining the table—how clueless can you get?*

So, are we talking about a problem of outlook? An issue involving the soul? No. Just look at Mina's parents, who are no better off than average in terms of ambition and culture. Strictly speaking, they might be slightly below average. Mina's mother graduated from a costly private university with a sprawling campus in the central city. She was active then in the anti-government and women's liberation movements, and now she's an established professional woman. Does this prove she's cultured? No. All it means is that back then she was in step with the times, and even the songs that were popular then. She grew up during a time when European philosophy and revolution were more popular than European designer bags, but if she were a student now she would scrape to collect designer bags and still be happier than her peers. If only she hadn't had to wait for her golden years for fashion to seek her out. Which accounts now for her mad dashes to the duty-free shops in search of those European designer bags. She looks like the wife of a shallow parvenu, and she is happy. She believes a taste for fashion is wired into human nature; you can't resist it. It's human nature to find the stacks of itsy-bitsy dessert cakes topped with herbs and tropical fruit irresistible, and so she, being only human, cannot resist them, and strongly believes it's perfectly natural, it's only *right*. But is it possible for anyone endowed with a soul to enhance the quality of his or her life by investing a lottery jackpot in a speculative venture? We can't call that a human life; instead it's the life of a beast, a creature true to its instincts. It's only a primitive life, the *most* primitive life, surrounded by the trappings of humanity. Such a life has nothing to do with spirit or soul. It's the life of soulless, conceited people. People who try to excuse their depravity by declaring they don't live in expectation of criticism or praise and that they respect the lives of others. But that's dishonest. In this world there is one kind of life that is worthy of criticism: the life of the depraved grown-ups. On the other hand, there is a life so pure it's impossible to critique: Crystal's life. Crystal is absolutely pure and undeniably perfect. Touting her absolute purity and perfection, she walks a straight and narrow path armed with a heavy brass shield and sword. But what if Paek Hanch'ŏl suddenly appeared from the bushes, hair covered with dust and dried leaves, wearing blue jeans from Kmart, offering her a tiramisu as soft as an angel's feather, and with an unaffected smile asked: *Why make your life a grind? It's not as if it's a war.* If that happened, Crystal would brandish the platinum credit card issued to only a select few by a leading global financial concern and sneer at him. Armed with that card she could pass through fifteen security checkpoints to enter a small restricted space with a sturdy desk and stiff chairs where she'd mingle with important people. She could do this forever or a night and come out absolutely clean. Eventually, she could come and go as she pleased, with or without the card (since her soul is like the chip in the card). She would refer to this as freedom, emphasizing *free*, and discuss the notion of freedom with other members of the flawless chosen. Needless to say you wouldn't find things like royal French dessert cakes there. Instead she would have tepid orange juice.

While Crystal is thinking about Mina, the bell for language class sounds and a group of kids pour into the classroom with the teacher. Pounding her lower back, the teacher calls out the page number they'll start on. Right hand holding her pen, left hand propping up her chin, Crystal continues to dwell on Mina:

Mina doesn't like British rock. She doesn't like Thom Yorke from Radiohead because he's an elitist, a graduate of the prestigious University of Exeter; she doesn't like Oasis because they're arrogant; she doesn't like Suede but can't tell you why; and she doesn't like the Beatles because they suck. Fed up with Mina slamming her one and only Thom Yorke, Crystal once said: So what, your favorite group, U2, are British too, aren't they? Mina listened silently, then burst into tears, fled to her room, and locked herself in. The next morning at school Mina told her that U2 aren't British, they're from the great nation of Ireland, and to prove it she handed her a printout from a site she'd Googled. Flustered, Crystal shouted at her to go to Ireland and not come back since *obviously* she was Irish. Mina proceeded to leave fifty postings on Crystal's Ssai World page, each of them reading *Yeah, I'm Irish*. Remembering now how sore her thumb had been from having to remove all fifty posts, Crystal prayed Mina would get locked in her closet and never come out.

Her family will be gone on vacation; they won't be coming back for three weeks! Outside the closet the phone will ring. Some of the calls are from me. But she can't answer. She's scared, she's pounding on the door, she's hungry—she's dying in there…

Crystal puts down the pen and scratches her leg.

Once she starts bawling in despair, ta-da, *here comes Crystal, and that's when I'll save her. Then we'll have a serious talk. I'll tell her I'm sorry I said I was sleepy when she was telling me about Chiye, and she'll say she's sorry she's been neglecting me. Then she'll say it's okay for me to go out with Minho, and then we'll make up. Hmm, haven't seen Minho in ages… Why am I so fixated on him? I wonder if he's getting along with his girlfriend. And if… Maybe he likes her more than me? Maybe she's prettier? I wonder how old she is. Is she tall? Can't Minho and I at least be friends? Whatever. It's all good. It's fine. It's great. It's all going to work out!*

Somehow she feels better. She picks up her pen, straightens in her seat, and gives her teacher a big smile. Not knowing how to take this, he says "therefore" when what he really wants to say is "so." Blushing at his blunder, he looks out the window then comes back with "so," and clears his throat, looking at Crystal again. She's still smiling. In a gentle voice he reminds the students to raise their hand if they want to ask about anything they don't understand. Instead the kids clamp their mouths shut and look down at their textbook to avoid his gaze. The teacher instructs a boy to explain the meaning of the bold word in the second line from the bottom of page 52. Burying his head in the book, the boy doesn't answer. The teacher opens his grade book and jots down a red X next to the boy's name. And with that the bell sounds to signal the end of class.

Crystal leaves the classroom as fast as she can. She puts on her headphones and turns up the volume. Out the classroom, out the school building, down the steps to the playfield, and across the field. *Where are the kids who would take me in their arms for the price of a smile?* Not spotting any takers, choked with loneliness, she scowls and thinks more about Mina.

Crystal goes into Mina's apartment. From the end of the hallway comes faint light and noise from the television. Minho, wrapped in a blanket, lies on the sofa playing a video game. She decides not to say hello. Minho raises a hand in greeting anyway, then puts it back beneath the blanket.

"Nice nap?"

Mina opens her eyes to find Crystal standing over her. Crystal bends down to have a look, but Mina closes her eyes and pulls the quilt over her head. Crystal pulls it off.

"Sorry," Mina murmurs, eyes still closed, "I thought you were a ghost."

"Let's go get some cheesecake."

Without a word Mina gets up and leaves the room. Crystal perches on the edge of the bed and sighs. She discovers a strand of Mina's hair on the sheet, takes an end in each hand, and pulls. The hair snaps.

"Having fun?" Leaning against the wall, Mina pours soymilk to the brim of a pink bowl half full of Crunch cereal.

"Why didn't you show up at school?" Crystal asks, looking in turn at Mina and the closet.

"I couldn't get to sleep last night so I took a sleeping pill. When I woke up it was one in the afternoon. Can you believe it?"

Crystal looks at Mina with an expression of utter disappointment.

"Why the look?"

"Tasty?"

"Yeah, you want some?"

"No, I'm good. But why is it so chilly in here?"

"Something's wrong with the heat. The other apartments have the same problem. Earlier it was crazy hot."

"So how about cheesecake?"

"Can't—tutoring time."

"Can't you skip it?"

"Don't want to."

"Not even for cheesecake?"

"Nope."

"Cheesecaaake…"

"I really don't want to go out, all right?" Mina gives her a hard stare that says, *You're being really annoying.* "It really, really sucks not being able to sleep."

"Cake…"

"I just can't get to sleep."

"So take a pill."

"You're not supposed to take sleeping pills every night."

"Why not?"

"Well…it's not good for you, right?"

"Don't ask me.… What does Minho say?"

"That idiot? He said not to take them, told me to throw them away."

"How come?"

"Don't know. Probably because he doesn't have trouble sleeping, the shithead!"

"Look, I've been dying for cheesecake—ever since I got up, and all through school."

"I'm going to go crazy if I don't get some fucking sleep. What if I can't fucking sleep, just can't, can't, can't fucking sleep, can't fucking get to sleep until I have a heart attack or something?"

"Have you always had this problem?"

"Yes!"

"I don't get it."

"I'm going out for a smoke."

"Don't leave me."

"Why not?"

"Don't, Mina."

"Why can't I?"

"Mina…I've missed you. Stay here."

Mina smirks.

"What's up with me today?" says Crystal.

"Nothing—you're always like this."

"How long since you slept?"

"Three days. I've slept maybe three hours in all that time."

"Something's wrong."

"I just can't get to sleep."

"That makes five times you've said that."

"So?"

"Just saying."

"It scares me that I can't sleep."

"So try to turn off your mind. And take a sleeping pill."

"Yeah? Are you sure?"

"Yeah."

"I just can't sleep."

Crystal looks at Mina. Mina looks at Crystal. Hesitantly Crystal asks, "Is it because of Chiye?"

"Look, why don't you go home."

"I knew it—you're still bothered by Chiye, aren't you?"

"You talk like I'm a hot air balloon or something."

"Ha, I'm right. Look at you, Mina, you're pissed. Why not just tell me—I'm all ears, I've been wondering."

"Shut up."

"Mina, don't. Just tell me. I want to know."

"Shut up."

"Mina."

"I said shut up."

"Mina, please."

"Oh my god." Mina plops down and starts pulling at her hair.

Putting her hand on Mina's shoulder, Crystal says, "I'm only asking about what's going on with you since Chiye. As your friend, a good friend, I want to know what her death has been like for you. Did you go to her funeral? Or maybe it hasn't been long enough? I know you probably feel rotten. Look, Mina, I—"

"You know something? You're really cruel."

"What? Sorry, I didn't catch that, what did you say again?"

"You're really cruel."

"What?"

"Mmm."

"Cruel? To you? Now?"

"Mmm."

"I'm cruel? Me? How? Why would you say that? I'm cruel? No, I'm just being honest. Cruel? Me? Really? You really think that? God…that's not…God…I…look, Mina…" With a sad look Crystal considers Mina, and the next moment she bursts like lightning: "IfyoufeelIambeingcrueltoyou Iamsorrysorrytrulysorryreallysorrysorrysorrysorry."

A hand on her forehead, Crystal slowly leaves Mina's room. Minho is sleeping, game controller in hand. Crystal is dejected. Mina follows her out, rests a hand on her shoulder, and says something, but it doesn't register. Crystal looks at Mina and shakes her head.

Crystal skulks from Mina's apartment. She gazes glumly at the fenced-in park where there's a sign saying For Residents Only. The healthy fruit trees, fresh grass, and large dog splayed out are like a glossy photo in a brochure. While traversing the zigzag path among the black locust and cherry trees bursting with blossoms, she comes to a stop, smothered by the scent. Looking up at the sky she murmurs, "It figures—the whole world hates me."

The sunlight is brilliant, the clouds pure white.

"I'm sorry."

And she hurries off.

And the beautiful path soon comes to an end, replaced by concrete and dusty, cracked asphalt, which jump out at her with stark clarity. And suddenly she feels something gigantic and oppressive. She tries to calm herself with comforting images—a department store on a lazy morning—but it doesn't help. Something is writhing and surging in her throat. She shudders. She feels tremors, chills, something weighing her down. Hand covering her mouth, she looks desperately for a garbage can. There's one nearby, so dirty she normally wouldn't be caught dead going near it. Closing her eyes tight, she leans over it, mouth agape, and pours out what's inside of her. Amid the utter darkness behind her tightly shut eyes and the reek of who-knows-what decomposing, she remembers the time she was hit with food poisoning. She tries as best she can to shunt the recollection aside, but the wretched memory only makes her feel more wretched now. Eyes still closed, she gropes her way to a bench and collapses onto it. When she opens her eyes she sees the sky above. A beautiful sight, almost too much for her with its vivid blue and endless variety of clouds, some reaching out slender arms and others layered like whipped cream on a canvas by Monet. The late afternoon sun dyes them a pastel peach. She notices a dark lump approaching from the distance. Slowly she closes her eyes and opens them. Nothing has changed. She repeats the action. She senses a massive amount of moisture coming to envelop the city. She hauls herself to her feet.

As she drifts around with no sense of direction the low clouds quickly cover the sky and before she knows it rain is pouring down. Instantly the streets turn into dark, damp, amorphous shapes like the sea on a storm-driven night, rain filling the places now emptied of people. Murky faces are reflected in streaming, rain-slicked shopwindows. Gusts of wind shred and scatter whatever is left on the street. Her arms clutched around herself, she takes refuge in a phone booth. In the next booth a man in a gray raincoat is talking on his cellphone. He looks up at the sky with a frown. Crystal turns her gaze to the pay phone in front of her but can't think of whom she ought to call. Emerging from the booth, she flags a cab.

The taxi cruises like a submarine beneath a dark and silent ocean. The unpleasant dampness pervading the city clings to her. Clings persistently to all of her and all of the city. She tries to immerse herself in other thoughts. First comes the phone booth, and then the garbage can, rain, *kimpap*, vomit, woods, canned coffee from a vending machine, more woods, a boot camp for kids, and finally food poisoning—her innermost recollections of utmost humiliation.

Once the girls arrived at the educational boot camp an instructor in his mid-twenties who wore a khaki cap and orange T-shirt tore into them: they had thirty seconds to assemble on the training field. Slowly unstrapping and dumping their backpacks, the girls gathered on the field, faces half smiling and half tense. The instructor blew his whistle and the students rolled, head over heels and then side to side, and by the time they'd covered fifteen feet their nice white tracksuits were covered with dirt. Next the instructor ordered them to their feet, in horse stance. Crystal was swept with zeal: *I'll show him*. She felt energy flow into her and got into a perfect horse stance. "You ladies are no longer little weaklings whining at your mommy's breast—forget that. In three days I'll remake every last one of you ladies, I guarantee it. So get moving. And don't think—I'll do that for you. Move!"

Crystal was singled out for praise by the instructor. The other girls dutifully applauded her. The joy she felt was complex—part furtive frenzy and part bashfulness—and it suited her just fine. It stayed with her for all three days as she tumbled around on the ground. Rebirth, love for her parents, facing life and coming out on top, comradeship, and all the rest—for three days she immersed herself in these thoughts, recording them in her diary to be treasured forever. Even as she stuffed herself with poorly steamed government surplus rice and radish kimchi that had gone bad, she thought, *Wow, am I cool or what?* Some of the girls got by on canned coffee from the vending machine for the first two days, but came down with stomach problems and spent the last day whimpering. Laughing at them, Crystal stuffed herself with *pulgogi kimpap*. But it was the other girls who had the last laugh, because the beef-filled rice rolls turned out to be spoiled. The first symptom was a faint rash on Crystal's face. Next came a stabbing pain in her stomach. She got a high fever and kept throwing up. The chunks of unsavory radish, the spoiled beef, and the rice gushed out of her in the order they'd gone in. Face positioned over a scummy garbage can, she sobbed. Three fervent days had climaxed with spoiled *pulgogi kimpap*, and she crashed and burned. What did she get out of those three days? Toned calves, freckled cheeks, food poisoning and its aftermath, the school authorities' cold, mechanical handling of her experience, and humiliation…that was all.

The rain continues to fall and Crystal comes to realize she's been preoccupied with misguided notions. The taxi moves sluggishly through the dark and the water but the meter moves rapidly. Suddenly she hates the driver, wants to kill him. *Not good*, she tells herself. Maybe she's too deep in bad memories. She always tries not to think too much. Because she knows if she looks deep down into her memories and sees the shame and humiliation, she'll end up killing herself like Chiye. She has to learn to look away from unnecessary thoughts at all costs. *Come on, girl, you need to love yourself, you need to stand tall and respect yourself.* She sits up but can't shake off the memory of the food poisoning.

Crystal's enthusiasm for the ultimately humiliating boot camp training should come as no surprise, because she's a perfect fit for institutional life. She's like a nice little white mouse in a tiny silvery cage, a person who wears the same colors and eats unpalatable food and sleeps on a hard surface in a tiny space—the perfect specimen for life within an organization. Every day the city builds higher walls for its institutions and she has no interest in escaping that world. Her only wish is to reach the summit, to rise so high that no one will take her lightly, so high that she can take others lightly. She wants everyone else underfoot so she can call down and tell them they can't come up. For that to happen, the institutions need to become even more institutional and the schools need to continue being the red-hot gates of hell. The teachers must continue to teach the students the virtues of submission and conformity. The world must continue to separate the ones who kneel from those who make them kneel, and to nurture, promote, protect, and advertise that distinction. Crystal has no interest in kneeling and isn't about to learn how. She doesn't want to be ordered around; she wants to be someone who doesn't follow orders. More precisely, she doesn't want to know what it means to follow orders; she wants to be someone who couldn't follow orders even if she wanted to. She knows that if someone laughs at her it's out of jealousy. The same goes for those who hate her. She knows that…knows it all too well. How then would she explain the sour sense of humiliation she feels deep down inside? Before she arrives at an answer the taxi pulls up at her apartment complex. She opens the door. The rain continues to pour down.

Dripping water she enters the apartment and makes her way from her bedroom to the living room to the kitchen to the bathroom, removing a layer of clothing at a time, and then, with a bath towel wrapped around her, she collapses onto the living room floor. The sky beyond the window is dark and menacing. The newscasters on the television keep reminding viewers that the rain will continue for days and that it contains more than the usual amount of heavy-metal particles. Crystal checks the clock on the wall. Time for cram school. She has to get up if it's the last thing she does.

THE LIFE OF A P CITY STUDENT

Crystal's confidence is not entirely of her own making. It's officially acknowledged by others and reflected in her writing. Thanks to the long years she's put into the writing class at the English Academy, her writing is extremely efficient, with well-constructed and compelling themes and flawless grammar. Superfluous conjunctions and punctuation? Forget it. She's talented at ferreting out sentences that deviate from the main point and subjects that don't agree with predicates. Her numerous compositions differ in detail but are alike in their emphasis on eliminating any content that falls short of exhibiting her extreme efficiency: Get rid of traditional methods that are no longer advantageous, avoid writing about experiences from which no lesson can be learned. She's a wizard at working within guidelines to organize and reorganize content; she's a virtual human printing press. Anybody who reads her compositions attests that nothing in them could merit a point deduction. Her writing always earns high marks, because the readers focus only on her perfect grammar and polished construction, particulars of that sort; they don't bother with her argumentation. And so her theses are often rickety in their logic and laughably paradoxical, but she couldn't care less. In her mind, the process is the point, and if no problems crop up along the way, then what's there to be concerned about?

The important thing is: Can this be applied to the here and now? Considering this sentence she's just jotted down, Crystal thinks, *Wow, you're something, girl.*

Applicability…as in compatibility. Is this plug compatible with IBM, Samsung, and LG? In Crystal's view, whatever is inapplicable about the past is a mere relic to be discarded or refabricated.

Because she has had no experiences to speak of, the notions she's equipped herself with for academic writing are all she has…they're Crystal herself. It's amazing how well she can expound in English upon Rousseau, using the appropriate tenses, prepositions, and proper nouns with correct pronunciation and intonation. *And now let's get it down on the computer—start with Rousseau, get the tense right, use the correct relative pronoun, make sure the syntax is correct—everything in proper English.* The results of all this become her thoughts. It's not important whether she's actually *thought* about Rousseau, whether she likes Rousseau. What's important is whether she can talk about Rousseau (using the correct nouns), whether she can explain Rousseau's *Confessions* (using the proper tense), and whether she's acquired the proper accent, and the intonation and sound assimilation that go with it. So if she can jabber on about Rousseau with correct grammar in a New England drawl, she can convince others she's knowledgeable about him. The result? An exercise to satisfy standards of evaluation. And assuming the evaluator buys into this exercise, let's hear it for Crystal!

When Crystal prances through the street flaunting her highly refined contemporary Zeitgeist, students flock to her.

At first, still unsure of themselves, they sneer at her—just as Crystal, at least once in the past, sharing the same view they did, sneered at another. These students will probably cook up a way to question or challenge her. She'll respond with a cop-out or excuse, with irritation or disregard. And in the next instant the students will wipe the sneer from their faces and replace it with a look of respect. This is exactly what happens between Crystal and her followers, it's happening now, and it will happen in the future. They will end up respecting her. But Crystal will continue to disregard them, to treat them with contempt; she and the others cut themselves off from each other and are left with nothing in common. Identifying themselves by their age, which side of the tracks they live on, their gender, their parents' assets, what they eat, and what they wear, they lock themselves in compartments. Inside these compartments are spacious living rooms decked out with marble floors, the freedom to open up the doors to the balcony and the kitchen with its island and make them an extension of the living room, and, compliments of a central security system, a completely digital home. The sales pitch? Simplicity is all: Let go of the view. Don't overthink. Move in straight lines and make your life more convenient. Live in a small circle…small is beautiful.

The more compartmentalized the life, the older we get, and the longer we live, the more confined this world becomes. Those in the rear compartments look toward the front but they don't know what they're looking at, while those in the front occasionally look back in relief. The greater the number of compartments, the wider the gap in human relations and the more similar the compartments between us. Confined in compartments of the same size, the same thickness, the same height and color and material, we shrink, despairing, each of us, from the same number of worries and the same volume of misunderstandings. And then people are used to separating themselves from others, locking their doors, lowering their blinds, and curling up as they age. Once in a while they'll crack a window and peep at the other compartments, but their door remains shut. They shout but no one hears. Out of shame they cover their faces and their mouths and they sob. From their pile of plastic knives they select one and slash the back of a hand, but they don't bleed. The ones who don't belong in the compartments linger outside the walls and grow old. We have two choices: remain outside for who knows how long, or be integrated into the world of compartments and confine ourselves inside them. There's no other alternative. The compartments are either *white* or *black*; there's no *gray*, so please don't bother looking for it. There's no in-between. There exist only walls with thick panels enclosing cells that divide and multiply without end.

The compartments, or more precisely the system they are a part of, directly influence the students' lives, but if you're a student who's concerned about the future in that system you won't be found within it. Saying this is the future they've selected, the students stick out their chests before squeezing into their compartment. The progressivism of the students who are still untainted will be crushed by the system's conservatism, but these students won't even realize they've already shot themselves in the foot. They will have nothing to inherit or hand down, no advice to give, none they want to receive. They'll want to disappear somewhere without a trace—and even if they don't want to disappear, that's how they'll end up. With nothing to show for it. Pure hearts are broken in this fashion, then they are integrated into the system. Once integrated, none of these individuals knows to look beyond her surroundings, none keeps the instinct to reach out to others. They don't want to belong anywhere, but they begin to conveniently take advantage of the system and would rather not realize how passive they are. In this way, alone as ever, not knowing to reach out, they're reborn as people who are perfectly individual and yet perfectly submissive to the collective. Taking only what they need, they adopt a lifestyle of shirking both responsibilities and rights—accepting the very life the collective demands of them. *I don't want the duties that come with a collective, it's no fair that they make demands on me just because I belong here. I want to be like an anonymous consumer—pay for a service, get my money's worth, grab the receipt, then go home and be left alone and go to sleep. Talking with other people wears me out, so please, leave me alone, please, please, even if it means I die a solitary and lonely death.* And even while facing that most wretched death, isolated and oppressed by the collective, they will close their eyes with a smile, believing they've braved the most isolated and individualized death, a death they chose of their own free will. But the smile is not theirs, it's that of the system, the system that has distorted their vision. Strictly speaking, it isn't a matter of actual life or death. But what we're describing as life and death recurs everywhere in the city—at this very moment people are slowly being drowned. No matter how desperately they try to keep their heads above water, the system and its rules slowly flood their hearts. The only way to resist is to retire their heart from service, and when that happens something dies.

This is precisely the tragedy of consumers who want convenience. They absolutely cannot protest a price hike at their favorite restaurant. Their only options are to find a place within their budget or to fish more money out of their wallet and pay up. And while people are extracting a bit more from those who can least afford it so that they can maintain their standing as consumers, boost their self-worth, and have a bit more for themselves, the system marches on.

When Crystal opens the narrow window and looks out, the image of a person who has opened a narrow window and is looking out appears. That image is the beautiful image of her mother, her mother's mother, that mother's mother, and so on through the generations, and it is the only possibility for revolution that is given to her. What we're calling revolution is not far off. Getting up early, that can be a revolution. That's what her discourse tutor said in order to convert Crystal to being a morning person. The tutor has a degree from a university in France and is well versed in modern Western philosophy. She completed an eighty-page thesis in French on the philosophical notion of the here and now, applying Lévi-Straussian social anthropology and Marxist-Lacanian left-wing psychoanalysis, but when it drew no interest she returned home in despair and dived into the discourse industry in P City. She feels at ease lecturing on Deleuze and Derrida to anyone from first graders to high school seniors. In her spare time she's translating her thesis into English. She's also considered Japanese but never Korean. She believes her thesis wouldn't work well in Korean. She believes that every language has its own circumstances, its own volition. She'll explain in Korean that Korean does not work well for the circumstances of her thesis. But most likely the writing in her thesis is simply a failure. A mess, a clumsy copy of French philosophers' writing littered with hyphens, dashes, quotation marks, and commas. It's imbued with the kind of claustrophobia and self-contradictions you find in Escher paintings, and although it's true to her life it never achieves the aesthetic accomplishment of an Escher painting and instead comes across as crude and convoluted.

This tutor is deeply impressed by the confidence in Crystal's writing and the energy with which she pursues a chosen topic, and she holds out special praise for the quality of its final draft. But what exactly is this quality? It's a package, that's what. It's like an elegant but strong glass container bearing a logo that makes you think it's French, with product information in five languages and the price listed in five currencies, and inside is an equal mixture of cheap mineral oil and glycerin. An intuitive interface between writer and reader, a simple and beautiful logo, a swift and pleasing context-driven exchange—this is what people mean when they speak of the quality of her writing. Among other things, Crystal's English Academy demands of the students this level of quality, and it's this quality, and all that's associated with it, that she's most confident in. She is a perfect, refined soul, with no rough edges that need smoothing, and although she's been feeling bored and numb for a while, so what? She is truly a soul of P City, which itself ranks high in finished quality, and so the residents of the city must welcome her presence with endless fanfare. Finally the city has borne fruit: the ideal human they've longed for is here! She's a highly distilled, one hundred percent P City soul. She is the most finished of students—look left and right, front and back, and see if you can find anyone better. What if we put her in a sterilized pouch made of some newfangled material and set her afloat on the ocean? She'd probably wash up on the shores of New England and find her way to an Ivy League school, where she would toss off a greeting before launching right into a discussion of Rousseau and the advent of the individual in modern society. Decked out in a beautiful dress and displaying a

sophisticated air, she'll make grand entrances at cocktail par-
ties. And at long last P City will have this refined soul whom
it can proudly plug into a glittering uptown shop window in
any city in the world, or into the background of a pop music
video. She is truly a new and improved type of human. She
can think in English with perfect grammar, she's beautiful,
she's free of depression, insomnia, and allergies, she's not trailing any shadows, and even as she leads those around her into
a gray area she'll still survive to the end with her head held
high. And because of her aesthetic perfection, we can't help
but be enchanted by her beauty. We're like backwater tourists
who, yet to be broken in by capitalism, are overwhelmed by
the offerings in the airport duty-free shops. She would be
at home anywhere, whether the ritziest of Dubai hotels or a
150-year-old apartment in Poland, and wherever she might
be she would adopt the same standard of living. But of course
she's not about to go anywhere for now. She knows, though,
that if she *were* to go somewhere, anywhere, life is fixed in
certain respects, and that the cost of living is based on a standard exchange rate—it's all straightforward. Around her neck
hangs a barcode and price chart listed in five currencies—a
survival strategy. And to survive, she leads a very hectic life.
She works like an ox and a horse combined, and when she's
not working she's carnivorous, feeding off others even as they
feed off her. When besieged by alcohol and greasy food, like
overworked office drones blowing off steam at the end of the
day, she smiles. Consuming and wasteful, crude and violent,
leaving their surroundings barren and desolate—this is the
life of the students in a city—a life often portrayed in doc-
umentaries as an adrenaline-fueled realm of risk and entice-
ment, a kingdom laden with rape and bullying, booze and
tobacco, violence and sex. Is it true that rape and homicide

are on the rise among young people? Is life getting worse and worse for kids? Was life a bed of roses for the previous generation? No one's talking, maybe that's the problem? Or maybe it's that everyone looks on the sunny side of the street and pretends the shadows don't exist? Or maybe it's simply that kids are watching too much porn?

A life bound by a few internet sites pushing information on the public all day long, and by a few flyers picked up at any subway station. A life where you're scheduled to go to a language camp in an English-speaking country and a ski camp during the long summer and winter school breaks. A life that can be summarized by an adequate command of English and appropriate people skills. This is the life that Crystal leads now and it's the life that awaits her. In the evening a mob of students, clutching pencils and cellphones, hovers outside the smoothie shop that just opened across from the cram school; their parents struggle to cover their expenses. Parents like Mina's and Crystal's, who have the ability to do this, are in the minority. These burdens are manifested in the huge digital clock at City Hall Plaza, whose golden letters and numbers are fodder for the parents, reminding them of what their duty is. Chewing on these figures, the parents weep in anguish and hardship. They inherently know that to be true residents of P City, even if they can't cover their children's expenses, they must at least pretend they can. Once a month they have to dine at a downtown restaurant that bustles with Westerners who add a tip and pay a surcharge. They love the vibrant ambience and are energized by the abundant varieties of fresh organic fruits and vegetables. The parents draw comfort from being able to cover what they must. Thus encouraged, their fighting spirit strengthened, they're ready to cover even more excessive expenditures. There's a peculiarity to this wave of esprit—it gets higher and higher, never subsiding, forever gorging itself on those who have drowned. This strange wave builds constantly, yesterday's crest giving way to today's even higher crest, so that yesterday's high water is suddenly the lowest of low water and barely an afterthought. People speak in muted tones about what they have to cope with: We have to cope with today because tomorrow there's even more we'll have to manage. Life is a matter of coping, and the most important thing is to survive, whatever it takes. So in order to survive, we have to cope. Whatever comes up, we can't just shake our heads and say no. We have to silently accept it. We have to be content with meager wages, conflicted relationships, unfair treatment, and a wasted life. That way we'll have an opportunity to carry heavier burdens, and that's not a punishment but an reward. To live an advantaged life, we must cope with this reward along with everything else. For *reward* read *suffering*, and for *suffering* read *reward*. It's that simple. Life is a series of painful exchanges. The medium of these exchanges is P City's private tutoring industry, a colossus without precedent.

The residents of P City have access to the choicest education in the world, laid out right in front of them, an infinite selection of educational products starting with private tutoring and continuing with study-abroad programs or alternative schooling, ranging from elite day schools to boarding schools, stimulating the appetite with the same diversity of multinational offerings you'd find at your local Starbucks. The people of P City know how they should spend their money, at least as far as education is concerned. Be proud, they tell themselves, you belong to the most highly educated citizenry in the world, and therefore have the most rewards. As we've mentioned, reward means suffering and suffering means reward, and the effect of this quality education consists of only one thing: inflating their egos. Consumed by ego, they pursue a superstore lifestyle and if along the way the traditional markets, the old bookshops, and the neighborhood eateries get swallowed up, they can always shift the blame to corrupt politicians. They adopt a lifestyle of speaking a Western lingo others can't follow; they roam like a pack of dogs ravaging everything in their path; and when they're done roaming they get an exclusive luxury apartment in which they build their own private utopia. Never do they acknowledge there will be a price to pay. They're already paying the price. Their inflated egos have already burst but they're unable to let them go, so they shoulder them on a journey through a tunnel of suffering. For them the world is no longer normal. Rats will abandon clean water and swarm to the pot where sugar water is mixed with heroin. Not because they're addicted but because they need to numb the pain of their distressing lives and block out the torment.

If you find yourself crying because your ego prevents you from giving up on something you can't afford, don't despair—everyone else is in the same boat! So what you do is put on your most snobbish look and pick up something even more expensive, or go all out and get the most expensive item of all. Let your ambition run wild. Aim higher. Do that and you'll end up with a bonus—a pair of fancy speakers or the cellphone your favorite celebrity uses. That's how you get to the top of this pyramid—but all that awaits you there is an exorbitantly priced dinner, an exorbitantly priced espresso, and an exorbitantly priced apartment, nothing you wouldn't find at the top of other pyramids. So what's new?

People often say that advantages bring disadvantages, that actions are accompanied by reactions. It's only natural that there are dark shadows, but in P City, anyway, such expressions don't make sense. If you're going to describe this city correctly and precisely, you have to phrase it something like this: an immensely inflated disadvantage brings a bit of an advantage. It's identical to drug addiction. The greater the pain when you wake up, the more intense the moment of pleasure at that first hit. When your brain is conditioned for the pinnacle of pleasure, your body is too weak to remember the pain. With all the suffering that's already around you, it's not easy to distinguish the suffering from the addiction from the other kinds of suffering. And so you tolerate it. You confuse the suffering that comes from addiction with the suffering that comes from life. But you never get used to it. Instead you convince yourself that life is a process of progressive pain and you grin and bear it. People extol the sliver of light that sometimes penetrates suffering—*hope remains*, or *that's the human spirit at work*—but any sliver of light is merely a momentary delusion of the late-stage addict. It's an anomaly, how could it be anything else? What's normal about searching for hope amidst suffering when the world all around you has gone crazy? As the waves crest higher and higher, who wants to stay where the water is lowest, defenseless and defeated, consigned to oblivion? Instead you try to escape. You have to run. There's nothing brave about going toe to toe with the waves that will surge over you. Just take off, screaming, as far as you can go, follow the mad rats that are following the pied piper. There's no time to lose. People are already submerged, bodies in the water.

In the end, life will smother Crystal. She'll be all by herself then. She won't be able to do a thing. In the end the foulest things you can imagine will taint her. She'll be stripped of all that she cherishes most. That's how she's been raised: by conquerors.

And this is how she'll survive. Hitching a ride on the backs of mad rats, she will survive. She'll reign triumphant. Crushed to death, she'll send out a beacon of light from the top of the highest tower—smothered yet shining.

This is Crystal's situation to deal with now, the society and the space in which she lives, and there's no way around it.

CRY AS MUCH AS YOU CAN

There's been no letup to the rain, but there are still sandy layers of dust in the sky. The television warns of global warming and red tide. Dampness rules the city. Women's hair has lost its curls and hangs limp, and tortilla chips lose their crunch as soon as the bag is opened, so they need to be toasted before being eaten—it's that kind of weather. The patter of falling rain clings to the ear like a song that won't go away.

But now that the rain has finally stopped and the sun has returned, the world, revealed in its dazzling light, looks somehow transformed. The weather has warmed up enough to melt butter and soften cheese. It's Wednesday morning and under the clear skies Mina and her mother are visiting her soon-to-be-former school. Wearing street clothes instead of her school uniform and sporting dark glasses and headphones, Mina walks with her eyes front, not greeting anyone. Her mother is dressed in a pink spangled blouse, a green chiffon skirt, and gilded spike heels, and accessorized with a gold-colored saddle bag. Her face is agleam with perspiration and foundation. She looks glum and seems preoccupied. Ripples pass through the monotone sea of school uniforms, the iridescent mother and daughter drawing everyone's eyes.

Into the school office they go, the students massing outside. While Mina's mother signs the withdrawal form and talks with her homeroom teacher, Mina remains zoned out behind her dark glasses and headphones. One of the other teachers approaches the table where Mina is sitting and offers her a can of mango juice, but Mina waves it off. The teacher leaves the can on the table and disappears. Head bobbing, shoulders shimmying, singing in a soft, low voice, Mina takes the can, pops it open, and sips. Her mother looks at her, absolutely baffled, then lowers her head and yanks at her hair:

"How in God's name did I end up with a kid like her?"

"Excuse me?" says the homeroom teacher.

Mina's mother bolts up, marches over to Mina, and slaps her on the shoulder in irritation. Startled, Mina springs to her feet. Mother and daughter leave the office. The students disperse, murmuring. A blinding ray of sun suddenly shoots through the hallway, and everyone looks away, squinting. Mina's mother hoists her gold-colored saddle bag to block the sun. Mina in her dark glasses is the only one to keep her eyes forward; her expression is unchanged. Mina and her mother slowly walk past Crystal. But Crystal doesn't approach; she gives no hint of recognition. She looks at Mina but can't see if Mina in her dark glasses is looking at her. Before she can ask herself what's happening, Mina and her mother have left the building. But she feels neither sorrow nor shock, only as if some trivial clump of gray matter buried deep in her brain has eroded—one more useless appendage has atrophied and dissolved, that's all. Such tiny erosions have been occurring for some time now. Craving sugar, she hurries to the snack bar for dark chocolate studded with espresso beans, then paces for a few minutes before heading out to the pine grove beyond the playfield. As she ambles along she thinks about the minute clump in her brain that's eroded. But instead of gathering, her thoughts keep scattering. About to cry she looks up, and there in front of her is Mina. Registering Crystal, Mina slowly removes her dark glasses and headphones. The sun has made a lemonade-colored halo around Mina, which is so strong that Crystal can't distinguish Mina from Mina's long shadow stretching out toward her. Long dark Mina approaches her.

"Mina."

Crystal notices Mina's bloodshot eyes and the dark semicircles beneath and takes a step back.

"What's wrong?" asks Mina.

"I'm scared."

"Scared of what?"

"Your shadow is so long."

"Let's go in the woods."

They sit beneath a tall pine and for a while they don't say anything.

"Crystal, I don't want to keep living. What should I do?"

"Yeah, I'm not exactly thrilled about life either."

"What do you mean? You've got a boyfriend. You've got a lot to live for."

Watching Mina, Crystal searches for a reason for her to live. But nothing comes to mind. Flummoxed, she wonders if that means it's all right for Mina to die.

"No, I can't say I do. Look, Mina, didn't you make it this far because you had something to live for?"

"I don't think so. I've never really thought about stuff like that."

Crystal dabs at Mina's tear-wet cheeks.

"I just want to die."

Mina is crying harder now. Crystal looks at her face.

Then she looks up at the sky. Fuzzy white light. She feels dizzy. Again she looks at Mina's face. Mina crying, her face rose red, and she's beautiful. It's a feeling she can't deny. She reaches out and pulls Mina close. The scent of the pine needles pierces her nostrils. The odor of cool earth, the scintillating light, the tangy pine scent, the tepid air with just the right humidity—they all come together to deliver a powerful boost to Crystal's spirits. Slanting shafts of radiant light fall all around, and she and Mina are right in the middle of it. Mina's polo shirt feels cool and crisp and gives off the fragrance of soap. Her hair streaming down is framed by the needles. Crystal nestles her head against Mina's chest, taking in the soap fragrance and the scent of pine needles. She's drowsy, wants to hang on to this time and space a little longer. The needles quiver faintly in the breeze. The girls embrace for what feels an eternity, like lovers caught in a storm, clinging in quiet desperation.

Crystal hears the distant ring of the bell for the start of class. She can't tell if the ringing is real or if it's coming from inside her head. She doesn't want to know.

Mina gives her a gentle prod. "Time for class."

"Yeah."

"I've got to go." Wiping her tears, Mina puts her dark glasses and headphones back on. Crystal gazes at her blankly.

"I'm off. Bye."

"Bye. Be safe."

With a wave to Mina, Crystal runs off. Behind her glasses Mina is crying. Crystal doesn't look back as she runs toward her classroom. She takes the bar of chocolate, unwraps it, and bites. The oh-so-rich and bittersweet chocolate combined with the dry crunch of the coffee beans envelops her in a sense of loss. She feels she's tumbling down an endless flight of stairs, like someone with an ulcer who's chugged a super-sweet mug of cocoa. These are new sensations for her. Something has come to an end. A thread has been snipped, a door closed, and she realizes now that there's a place to which she can never return.

The earth is turning too fast. If she's not careful she'll end up flying off toward the far side of the universe.

Feeling a tremor from the ground, she lurches to a stop. Gingerly she lifts a foot and sets it down. Nothing—no movement beneath her sneaker. She looks up at the sky again. The sun is hiding behind a baguette-shaped cloud.

She feels the loss deeply, is momentarily breathless. A throng of students storms toward her, then they pass by, giggling and talking. It's nothing, she keeps telling herself as she starts up the steps of the building toward her classroom.

Mina's gone, she's disappeared, she hasn't come back. And Crystal's not about to go looking for her. Words don't pass between them any longer. Crystal tries to forget her, but the feeling of loss won't let go. It's like an abandoned well, a place she passes by all the time until one day she falls in. The well is bottomless. It has nothing to do with the laws of physics, and yet she falls vertically, a slow and steady drop. The stone wall of the well is sometimes gray, sometimes black, maybe even orange, but mostly it's colorless. She's still dropping and there's still no bottom. But she's surely falling, and that's the problem. *How can I be falling down when I didn't have enough time to reach the top?* The rock wall is cold and hard and damp to the touch. She hears cheerful reggae music in the distance, is reminded of the sweet smell of grass. Time passes and she starts getting bored, but she still can't release the tension she feels. And now, finally, she's getting angry. But still she's dropping. She tries to think rationally—there has to be a way to overcome this, there's got to be a lesson to learn. But the next moment she feels stupid—she might as well try to coat this stone wall with egg white.

What do I do now?

Great—she's asking herself the same question Mina asked her and never got an answer to. It's the same question but all it does is repeat in her mind; she's not troubling herself over it. These days, to keep up her English she's watching *Saturday Night Live* without the subtitles, one episode per night, watching it more than once, and she's gotten to where she laughs along with the live audience. Occasionally she'll feel she's really getting the hang of American humor, but she's not sure if this is a kind of default brainwashing that results from all the work she's put into studying English, or if she's laughing because the jokes really are funny. The more ambiguity she has to contend with, the angrier and more fretful she becomes. And before she knows it a primeval anger has taken over—especially when, for the umpteenth time, she hears a word she doesn't know. That's when despair hits and she kills the TV and turns on music, jacking up the volume. She dances and she shakes her head every which way and she tries to roust all the unpleasant thoughts.

Damn these thoughts—get lost! But it doesn't work.

Give it up, girl. Shut up unless you want to cry.

Now it's the music she kills out of anger, before going to her room. She sits at her desk and flips open her math workbook and she's off and running. The first problem involves a graph and simple trigonometry. There's a simplicity and an exquisitely logical beauty to the structure of a math problem. There are several steps, each one involving at least one formula but no more than three. Once you've got the important numbers in front of you, you move on to the next step. The higher the degree of difficulty, the more steps you face and the harder it is to get a grip on which among the range of formulas you need to apply. Among these steps, for the hardest problems, you'll need a revelation from the math god in order to find a clue to the solution. You can think of it as creativity. In any event, the map is simple. But numerous students end up losing their way and losing hope trying to follow it. Crystal kind of wishes that with a stroke of his wand the math god would hex those pathetic students so that they'd forsake the road to wealth and power and take up a practical skill instead.

Mina sucks at math. Crystal looks down on her for that. But still she loves her.

She's on the third problem when her cellphone rings. She picks up, gives a grudging nod, and hangs up.

Pyŏl is sitting on a bench having a smoke. He sees Crystal and grins. Crystal plops down on the ground in front of the bench.

He gets up. "Have a seat. It's warmer."

"No, I'm fine."

He sits back down.

Head down, she passes her fingers along the ground. "You said you had something to tell me?"

"No."

"Then what?"

"Just… I miss you, that's all."

"You miss me… So?" She looks up at him. "What's that supposed to mean?"

"'What's that supposed to mean'—what are you trying to say?"

"I'm just asking. I mean…isn't that kind of vague?"

"I heard C has lung cancer." He bends forward and grabs her wrist.

"How old is he?"

"Twenty-three."

"You've got to be kidding."

"No lie." He sighs, sending out a stream of smoke. They lapse into a black silence.

"I need to quit smoking."

"How old were you when you started?"

"Seventh grade."

"That's a long time."

"Crystal, you should quit too."

"Why?"

"Girls are fragile, don't you know?"

Crystal thinks about Mina. Pyŏl crushes out his cigarette. She picks a flyer up from the ground and starts ripping it.

"What're you doing that for?"

"Mind your own business. I'm not quitting. I'll die of lung cancer. When I'm twenty. I don't want to live any longer than that." She's talking louder, her voice lovely, high-pitched but gentle. Pyŏl considers her, not sure what to do. She sticks a hand in his pocket and rummages around.

"What're you doing?"

"I want a cigarette."

"In there." He points to his bag.

"Shit." She takes a cigarette and lights it. "It's so irritating."

"What is?"

"I don't know. And that makes me more irritated."

"That's life."

"Not my life."

Mina and her family moved.

She transferred to an alternative school.

Or she's studying in France.

Or she went to Seattle.

Whenever rumors start flying, the students look at Crystal. Covering her ears, Crystal resorts to math problems in desperation—the subject Mina hates the most.

"Hey, Crystal, any news from Mina?" When the brave ones venture to question Crystal, she sticks out her tongue and says she's not telling. "It's a secret." And then she bursts into laughter.

Frightened, the kids back off.

Crystal is floundering; she's about to lose her balance. She promises herself she'll never, ever cry. Instead she takes up laughing. She watches American talk shows and laughs until she's crying. And then she's back in the well, falling, but still laughing. She looks up at the sky and laughs, looks down at the ground and laughs. But the moments of numbness when she doesn't cry or laugh are much more numerous, and it's those moments she loves the most. She yearns for numbness, when she's like a cold brick of butter or a rock-hard bagel, because that's when she's best at her studies.

In a state of perfect numbness she gets up, yells, kicks her desk, and exits the classroom. Five desks fall like dominos. Her classmates look toward the door with eyebrows arched and mouths agape. The bell rings for the next class. Muttering, the kids pick up the toppled desks. And then Crystal is back, along with the next teacher. Laughing as always.

<u>Okay, let's assume you do all that—in the end what difference would it make</u>? Crystal underlines this sentence

for good measure.

I'm having the time of my life and it's not stopping anytime soon. She underlines that sentence too.

AT 23:27:40

I don't like people. They're idiots, and I hate idiots. Why do people want to die? Because they're dumb. I don't understand it. I don't understand people. I'm practical and efficient and pragmatic. But other people aren't. It makes me mad. Unproductive and inefficient. It makes me mad. Stupid kids ought to be put to work on a farm. I mean, they only get four out of ten questions right! I don't get it. It tells you what kind of parents they have. Those kids are pathetic! So I want to kill them off. But I won't—what good would it do me? I don't mean to say smart kids are better than stupid ones. Smart kids want the lifestyle displayed in the department stores: go to a good university, work for a big company, marry a rich kid. But stupid kids don't qualify. You can't get that lifestyle by being good at workbook problems; you need a mind of your own, and that's one thing the stupid kids lack. So why bother living? I wish I could tell them there's no reason they should exist. Then kill them, a slow, painful death. After the job is done I'll have a good laugh. Imagine them becoming teachers—they'd dote on the kids who reminded them of themselves, but be jealous of the exceptional ones like me. The dean of students at my school hates me because I'm better than him. It's that simple. He has a one-dimensional mind. He keeps telling me that good grades by themselves are worthless—as if it's your personality that gets you into a university! He's wrong, it's not personality, it's percent-ality, it's all grades. What's more, all the best people are social misfits, they're mentally ill, they have personality disorders. No way do I want to just be adequate. I don't want to be just smart enough, or just good-looking enough. I'm not going to go along, not me. I'm going to be great.

The problem is: there are too many people who ought to be killed.

But if you think about it, the great ones have killed a lot of people. Greatness means you're bestowed the right to kill. Without it you can't be great. But there's a small problem—who do I kill first? Say I live to be a hundred, can I kill all the people I want? That's a pretty tall order. I have plenty of candidates right here in this country, so just imagine how many more there are in India and China. Dumb kids keep getting born, over and over and over— they multiply like cockroaches. More than anything I'm scared of bugs. Last night a weird bug came into my room, crawled up to the ceiling and back down to the window, and then flew off. That was all it took. I threw up. And while I was throwing up I was thinking about math. And about the booze and cigarettes I keep in the locker at the study-room my parents rent for me. And just then, surprise, out came a big hunk of sweet potato I ate yesterday morning. Nothing more to throw up, so back to my room I went. I sat at my desk and did more math, and I hit upon an idea—everybody ought to die. Last month my dad bought me a new set of speakers. The sound is so awesome I can't just sit and listen, I have to get up and dance. U2 is on now. Mina likes U2. I hate them. But I listen to them anyway. My dad's weird. When I came in first in my class he got mad at me for missing easy problems. This time I came in fourth and he bought me a new set of speakers.

I don't need anyone to smoke or drink with. I'm in bed and it's 1:14 in the morning. I love myself. But other people don't. They're afraid of me. I know that. No one could love me. I'm the only one who can really love me. There's no one else who could really love me. I should always remember that and never have second thoughts. And never trust anybody. Not even Mina, if she were still around. She shouldn't have been in the picture to begin with. Mom and Dad have no clue that I throw up. Occasionally I throw up. I take that back. I don't throw up. Ever. Last night was an exception. I hate living like this. No, actually I want to live like this. I just want to kill them all. That would be better. I'll finish my homework and go to bed now at 1:14. That works for me. The teachers make you stand out in the hallway if you don't finish your homework. Or if you're lucky you just lose some points. The days we have five classes instead of four, we get four break periods in between. I do my homework during second break and Chini copies it during the third while I'm on the phone with Pyŏl. First break, I take a nap. At lunch time I do my cram school assignments. During home ec I chat with Chini about makeup. Maximum efficiency in time management, see? I have no idea what the other kids do during break. The girls, all they do is breathe, anyway—they don't go out with boys and they don't study. Why don't they just turn into squid? Then they could at least be a part of my squid fried rice. And since I hate squid I could dump the whole thing. Those kids would be better off dead. Just looking at them makes me mad. Who wants to live their life being treated like shit? It's pathetic! I'd like to kill them but I'm too busy. Busy being great! I need to be fabulous! Hmm, maybe I'd be better off making money instead of killing people. Maybe I'd be better off stocking up on cosmetics. Or dumping the makeup I already have. Maybe anything would be better than killing people. But the fact remains—there are too many people in the world who ought to be killed. Some people have no reason to live. When people die, what happens to them? Do they get reborn as other people? That's a scary thought. If that's the only option, then our planet would be better off dead. And in that case I'm willing to die with everybody else. But that's not going to happen. Or it might. But it won't. But I hope it could. I hope the earth goes poof! *I want everything to end. Really. Seriously. No lie. Today was fun, sure it was. Today was fun, definitely. Today, definitely fun. Today was fun. Today was fun. It was fun. Fun. Fun.*

After deleting all this Crystal begins her homework composition. Twenty-four minutes later and it has reached the required length. She corrects the seven grammatical errors and then it's perfect. She hits Print. Reading the printout she knows she'll get a hundred. Off to bed she goes at 1:14, right on schedule.

THE CLOSET

In her dream Crystal is looking for a calendar, but it's no-where to be found. Then she goes outside to look for her fa-ther. He too is nowhere to be found. She phones her mother, but her mother doesn't pick up. Back home she finds the door locked. She calls Mina, but Mina doesn't answer either. Down scroll the numbers in her contacts list, only to disappear one by one off the bottom of the screen. Oh, there's the calendar. Through a window she sees the dates on it disappearing one by one. Screaming into her phone, she kicks at the door. No response. All she can do is sit outside the door, fidgeting, and at that point she awakens. The moment her eyes open, half the dream is gone. But the acute desperation lingers, freezing the near reaches of her heart and leaving her with an icy-cold pain. A fly buzzes around her unlit room in absolute leisure. She gets up, turns on the light, and sprays bug killer. The fly falls to the floor, belly up. Its legs tremble and then it stiffens. She frowns but can't look away. In her current state of mind she needs to take a walk. In the lobby, the elevator opens and her eyes are met by the sky streaked with red and blue. She raises her arm toward the sky then brings it down as if to usher in the darkness, the blue appearing to move with her arm. The clouds seem devoid of moisture, like seasoned firewood. It's the hour of afterglow, the day's demise, the sky bleeding to death. The thickness, intensity, and hue of the twilight change by the minute. It's an unsettling time of day for the heart and soul. The lonely weep, while the love-struck are reminded to call and whisper declarations of love. Crystal's defense against the unsettling sunset is to force a desperate smile and walk tall along the path through the apartment complex. The sky turns dark red as it dies. The silhouettes of tree branches bisect the sky. The wispy yellow light of the sky descends beyond the apartment buildings, and the bright yellow globes of the sodium streetlights come on amid the outlines of the dark trees. Like an exquisitely cut diamond, the sky changes hue by the minute. It's so beautiful. Crystal knows that, but because she can't feel it she looks away. The path is suffused with the warm glow of the streetlights blending with the last vestiges of sunlight. The glow of the shafts of artificial light is comforting. Arriving back at the entrance to the complex she lingers for a moment, and that's when she hears the faint meow. It's coming from a large box.

She opens the box and sees a gray kitten the size of her two hands cupped together. It meows, displaying milky fangs and a raspberry-red tongue. Without thinking she reaches for the kitten. It shivers, eyes half shut. Was that a breath of air she felt? The next moment it's gone. But the faint impact remains. She pets the kitten on the forehead and it twitches an ear, its mouth opening wide. She takes it from the box and holds it close. She can't believe how feather light it feels, a handful of fur and bone with a bit of warmth to it. Its paws—she could crush them if she tightened her grip—cling to her clothing with tiny sharp claws as it trembles. Why won't it stop meowing? She looks into its eyes. They're large, shaped like almonds, and have an olive glow. Crystal heads toward her building. The tiny thing is causing quite a fuss. The eyes of her neighbors as they pass by come to rest on Crystal. Some smile, some frown, but most are impassive. Smiling, she passes a hand through her hair and hums just loud enough for them to hear her. The kitten is still meowing and its fur is now standing up. "Nice kitty," she coos, but it won't quiet down.

"Are you afraid of me?"

She opens the door and sets the kitten on the living room floor. Prone, it gazes around warily, beginning to meow again.

"Hey, kitty, hush up."

She curls up on the floor and hums a lullaby, then reaches out and pulls the kitten toward her. Baring its teeth, the kitten bats her hand away.

"Ouch!"

The kitten's pointed tongue appears between its teeth and it hisses.

"Ooh, scary." Crystal bursts into laughter. She can't stop laughing. And as she laughs she feels anger infiltrating the laughter—more and more anger. She won't be able to stop, she tells herself. She's laughing compulsively but doesn't know why, rolling on the floor. And *what* is making her angry? Her laughter changes to hysteria. Her heart beats faster and she feels her musculature tightening. It hurts. She has to do something. She stops laughing, reaches for the kitten and covers its mouth with both hands. The kitten's head twists back and forth, its legs pumping, claws extended. A vivid red line grows on Crystal's arm. A smile pasted on her face, she starts hitting the kitten. A slight ticking registers in her consciousness, then recedes into the distance. She's barely aware of what she's doing, knows only that she can't stop, but then suddenly awareness returns. She puts the kitten on the floor.

"Oh, no!" She places a hand over her mouth.

Low to the floor, tail hidden, the kitten crawls under the coffee table.

"I didn't mean it."

The kitten bares its teeth.

"I didn't." She waves to it. "Hey, hey, hey. I didn't mean it, really. I'm sorry, kitty. I didn't mean it. I didn't mean it. I didn't mean it!"

There's a tense silence. Shoulders hunched, they glare at each other. The kitten is the first to look away. It lifts its left front paw and licks it.

"I didn't mean to hurt you…not at all." Crystal goes to the kitchen for something to feed the kitten. Through the window she sees the white of a half moon, tilted to the left. She imagines a woman's round shoulder glimpsed in subdued lighting. Gazing at the curvaceous moon, she lapses into thought.

I hope the planet dies. Before I turn twenty. If the planet dies then all the idiocy in the world can be saved—salvation from stupidity. In the meantime it's okay to be dumb. I can put up with idiots, sure I can. As long as the planet dies before I'm twenty.

She puts Crunch cereal in a shallow bowl, adds milk, and takes it to the living room. Where's the kitten? She gets down on the floor, looks around, and spots the kitten crouched beside the sliding door to the enclosed balcony. She yanks it by the tail and the kitten bites her on the wrist. Flinching, she lets go of its tail. The kitten hunches up in a ball, baring its teeth. She grabs it by the scruff of its neck, lifts it from the floor, and beats it with her fist. Clinging to her with its paws, the kitten tries to make itself smaller. It looks like a gray, withered persimmon hanging precariously from a twig. It yowls plaintively, sounding like fingernails scraping a chalkboard.

It's a feeble sound and it's lost in Crystal's panting. *Why am I breathing so hard?* She punches the kitten harder. She can't believe she's doing this. But then her mind reaches out into the distance and she recalls her half-forgotten dream. She tries to bring it into focus. Her fist crashing against the kitten's bones makes a peculiar sound. The crack of bone against bone gives her a momentary crude pleasure, a crass thrill that sends her falling down a stairway. The stairway is long and steep. Her free fall will last until she hits bottom.

Gasping for air, she manages to place the kitten back on the floor. She rubs her hand where the kitten has scratched it. She gazes dully at the kitten and a sudden, stupid grin escapes her. She pushes the bowl of cereal toward it. "Eat."

But it won't eat.

Crystal can't stop panting.

One more time she urges the kitten to eat. It turns and begins to slink away. She snatches it by the back left foot. The kitten yowls. She grabs its neck. With another yowl, the kitten scratches and then bites her arm. She hits it again and pushes its face into the bowl of cereal. It makes a gurgling growl, the milk bubbling. She lets go. The kitten sneezes and shakes itself, sending milk spraying in all directions, then wobbles and falls on its side. Crystal screams at it. The kitten hoists itself upright and crawls through the open door to the balcony. Crystal yanks the kitten's tail, dragging it toward her, leaving a diagonal line of claw marks on the floor. Eyes bulging, it scratches and bites her arm again. Vivid red blood oozes from her arm and forms into a trickle. With bloody fingers she picks up the bowl. The milk turns the color of strawberries. Again the little thing makes for the balcony. Again she snatches it by the tail. Blood drips from her arm to the floor.

"Eat."

It won't.

"Eat."

No.

"Eat!" she screams. "Eat! I said, eat!" She takes it by the neck and tries to force its mouth open. With its sharp teeth the kitten bites her index finger, rending the very tip of it. *Oh my god!* She drops it. A small chunk of flesh dangles from her finger. She pulls it free and blood paints the tip red. She turns toward the TV; the screen is dark and silent. She finds the remote on the couch and turns it on. A talent show she hasn't seen before. Cheered on by an audience of kids, fifteen boys with identical expressions bound onto the stage one at a time, do a dance number, then return to their seats. The same idiotic dance move, repeated fifteen times. Unbelievable. The boys are the same age as she is. They're like Pyŏl, so dumb they don't realize they're dumb. Cursing, she kills the TV. Wiping blood from the remote with her T-shirt, she returns it to the couch. She gets down on the floor, puts the injured fingertip in her mouth, and crawls toward the kitten. She's in a very nasty frame of mind and she knows it. She wants to wring the kitten's neck and break its legs. Everything has come together in nastiness. But why? Maybe it's because of the dream. She remembers the visceral sense of despair she experienced when she woke up, feels it embracing her again. The despair is suffocating her—she needs air. And that's when the rest of the dream comes back to her:

She's in an unknown city with a locksmith who had come to her apartment. They're traveling by subway but keep missing their stop. It's 9:20 p.m. and eventually the trains will stop running for the night. The locksmith suggests fifteen possible routes to get where they're going, all of them seemingly simple and straightforward but each involving transferring to a different line, and Crystal keeps missing the right stop. She decides to go with the man by bus to the subway station where they can transfer. It's 9:20 but the sky is as bright as day; the streets, though, are shrouded in gloom. They stroll along narrow sidewalks. She hears reggae music from a radio, at which point the man lies down on the sidewalk and with an innocent smile offers Crystal a white pill. Frowning, she shakes her head and takes a cigarette from her backpack. She helps the man to his feet as he smiles helplessly, then on they go. At an outdoor café bordered by a tiny brook they take a corner table. While he cleans his face in the brook she's delivered cups containing the dark crust of instant coffee, sugar, and creamer before she's had an opportunity to order. Filling the cups to the brim with hot water, she carefully stirs the mixture. Time stands still as she and the man sit at the café drinking the god-awful stuff. *Yuck—they still sell this?* Their chairs rest on muddy ground.

"It's nine twenty and the sun's still up," says the man.

Time stands still, it's still bright out, but Crystal feels gloomy as she thinks about the subway stops she missed. She opens a guidebook to this unknown city and unfolds a map. The city is bordered on the south by a fortress wall and the rest of it is enclosed by a river. The map shows the streetcar and subway lines. She looks around, trying to connect what she sees with what's on the map. Nothing matches. It's still 9:20—she remembers checking her watch in the dream—but that's all she remembers because that's when she woke up.

Crystal looks out the window. The white curvaceous half-moon is still there. Against the backdrop of the dark, forested hill a pair of orange lights flicker once and then again. She crawls toward the lights. They attack her with bared claws. She grabs the gray tail, her bloody hand smearing it. The eyes have turned to slits, the pupils dark. She throws the thing as hard as she can against the wall.

It makes a thud like a sandbag when it hits, then drops to the floor.

Stretched on its side, the kitten is dying a slow and painful death, like a goldfish out of water. Kneeling on the floor and watching the kitten, Crystal rubs its tummy. She blinks slowly and warm tears drop upon where she's rubbing. The olive-green eyes have lost their shine.

What have I done?

Crawling on all fours, she apologizes to the cat, chanting *sorry sorry sorry*. But for the kitten the end has come. She puts her hands around its neck and squeezes one last time, then wails as she lifts the kitten high and lets go. It hits the floor with the sound of a button that's come loose from a jacket.

Looking into the kitten's dull eyes, she pleads: "I'm sorry I wasn't good to you—now I know—how much I loved you—but you don't know that since you're dead."

The kitten keeps up a faint growl, its hind legs twitching feebly. Its skinny tail lies limp and its gray fur has lost its luster. A long, feeble moan escapes its mouth, followed by an ooze of white, foul-smelling mucus. Crystal pounds the floor and sobs. Then, with another round of *sorry sorry sorry* she chokes the cat again until the foul ooze gets on her hands. She rushes to the bathroom and gives her hands a thorough scrubbing with strawberry-scented soap.

Kneeling again before the kitten, she watches it lift its head ever so slightly to look at her. She observes the cat. Its olive-green eyes, so mysterious and beautiful, are vacant now. She dabs at her eyes then uses her cellphone to photograph the kitten and record a video to capture its faint growl. She plays the video again and again and again.

In the meantime the kitten is inching toward death. *Why does it have to take so long!* She feels frustration, boredom, and regret all at the same time. She has to get some sleep before cram school. As she smokes a cigarette an idea comes to mind. It's the best way but the most cowardly way. After crushing out her cigarette and spraying air freshener all around, she looks in the shoe cabinet, finds two sturdy plastic bags, and secures the kitten inside them. There's no resistance from the limp kitten. She can still hear its feeble moan and its squirming paws rustling the bags.

"Bye—safe journey—sorry." With these parting words she opens the window and tosses the bagged kitten out. To avoid hearing the impact she quickly slides the window shut and covers her ears, then curls up on her bed. She remains motionless until she finally falls asleep.

In her dream she awakens to find a tiny spider at the foot of her bed. Terrified, she jumps out of bed. The bug doesn't budge from the far end of the quilt. She inches toward it and taps her quilt, and the spider eases beneath it. She lifts the quilt and finds a dark hole inside of which a spider the size of her palm is weaving its web. She screams. Eight legs pumping, the spider scuttles down the hole. Small spiders appear, glinting in the dark like shiny black seeds, then gather in a line and crawl into the hole. Crystal puts the quilt back down. Then, clutching her desk, she throws up.

From her mouth comes a white, gummy, foul-smelling ooze. Head lowered, mouth wide open, pawing at the air, she blurts out something incomprehensible. She hears the kitten moaning faintly beneath the quilt. She begins to cry but what comes from her eyes is the same gummy white ooze. It covers her face and it stinks to high heaven. The moaning from beneath the quilt sharpens into a cry. A long thin leg covered with steel-like bristles pokes out. Closing her eyes, she puts her head on her desk, but still sees everything. The desk begins to tilt and slowly falls apart. She opens her mouth to cry out, but the white ooze clogs her throat, choking back all sound. The desk collapses, washing her down like a mudslide.

She stands before the mirror looking at herself. With the crumbled desk layered about her she looks like a chocolate cake. She wipes off the part of the desk that's encrusted on her thigh. White ooze trickles down her chin. The spider's huge leg glitters darkly beyond the mirror, its dark thin shadow extending to her foot. She gathers the fragments of the desk into a ball and rolls it under the bed. She hears it bump gently against a soft surface. The kitten yowls.

"I'm so sorry!" says Crystal, still oozing at the mouth. She hugs the kitten and sobs. "I'm sorry. I made a mistake. I'm sorry. I regret that I killed you, really."

The kitten claws her cheek and out comes the white ooze, wetting her neck and the kitten's face. The kitten tries to wriggle free. The spider's dark leg still glints on the bed. Everything's hazy. The space of real life is receding from her. She finds herself on a smooth wood floor that's shrinking little by little, shrinking at a consistent rate, but never reaching the vanishing point. Frightened, she clutches the kitten more tightly.

"Sorry. Sorry."

The floor is turning squishy like Jell-O. Crystal screams and the kitten falls from her grasp. It hits the floor and shatters.

"Shit!" Head arched, she yells skyward. A huge spider leg dangles, swaying, from the ceiling. The ceiling is swelling, it won't stop. She gathers the fragments of the shattered kitten.

"Damn!"

Blood gathers from where one of the fragments has sliced her palm. To her relief it's blood and not the white ooze. It's a deep gash and it hurts. The floor pitches gently. She cuts the floor open with the side of her hand and sticks her arm deep down inside. Something pulls on her hand, something big and black and flickering.

Awakening, Crystal gropes on the nightstand and finds her hand mirror. Good—none of that yucky white stuff on her face and neck. And no trace of a cut on her palm. She hops out of bed and lifts the quilt. Nothing. She heaves a sigh of relief. She passes her hands down her face, then goes to the bathroom and wets her face and hair with cold water. The whirring of the fan is *so* irritating. The bathroom window makes a loud rattle. She looks around with saucer eyes, then scurries back to her bedroom and examines the ceiling and desk, then checks under the bed. She gets back in bed and pulls the quilt to her chin. And then she hears the front door opening and her parents laughing. Silencing her breath, she strains to listen.

A bottle is plunked down on the dining room table.

Glasses are clinked together.

Her door is gingerly opened, then shut. Eyes closed tight, lying rigid, she silently recites a physics equation.

She hears her mother go into the master bedroom and shut the door.

She lifts the quilt and eases herself out of bed.

She hears the click of her father's lighter.

She's seized with a sudden thought: the planet won't die till she's 120 at the earliest. Nothing in the meantime, only the flow of time. *Get it?*

She hears clanking—something metallic. The window rattles. The ticking of the clock is *so* annoying—she removes the battery and puts it in a desk drawer, then gets back into bed. She hears her father hack and spit—he's just crushed out his cigarette. She hears a drawer being opened. *Pop*—a bottle being uncorked. *Glug-glug*—wine being poured. The footsteps of her mother returning from the bedroom. Her parents' soft laughter.

She hears the door to their bedroom close. And the creak of their mattress springs. The click of the light switch in the hallway. Her father's footsteps in the hallway. The windows rattling.

"It's really blowing."

"What was that, honey?"

"The wind."

She hears the clanking—yes, definitely metal. With every breath she takes she feels her hair rustle. She still hears the clock ticking. As her chest rises and falls, her clothes whisper against each other. She curls her legs beneath her and hears the crumpling of the quilt. Her ears are aching—too many sounds bang on her eardrums and they're too loud, all of them. She hears the TV—the roar of a soccer stadium and the feverish voice of the announcer. She eases out of bed, opens the door to her closet, crawls inside, and shuts it. She no longer hears anything.

The planet's not going to die, and neither are people. No way will there be a nuclear war. Sure there are wars going on now, but the planet's not going to die because of them. And if the planet's not going to die, who knows, I might get lung cancer at twenty-three.

Or get killed in a car crash. I'll grow old and ugly and make stupid mistakes. Everyone's going to laugh at me. I won't make it past forty-four.

She buries her face in her thick winter coat and curls up. Tears stream down her face. She notices a pungent lavender scent. Could this have been the state of mind that drove Chiye over the edge? She feels smothered. She wipes her tears then leans back against the wall. It pushes back gently and begins to vibrate almost imperceptibly. She reaches out, gropes at it—Jell-O.

What the... Is this another dream?

With her palm she tests the back of the closet. It's Jell-O all right, a soft, bouncy wall of Jell-O. She slices it with the side of her hand and it opens easily. Carefully she squeezes into the opening. It's pitch black and she can't see a thing but can tell from the smell that it's dark red Jell-O made from mixed berries. It's vast inside, feels like it could go on forever—no floor, no walls, just space. Hunks of Jell-O keep falling into her mouth. She's slowly floating in every direction—forward, up, down—sliding toward the middle of the huge Jell-O mass. Deeper and deeper she goes.

Nothing happens as she continues to slide.

And then, as she's chewing a hunk of the Jell-O, it hits her! "*That's* why you went into your closet, Mina! I get it—it's a fantasyland in here, so soft and warm."

She hungrily munches the Jell-O.

"But it doesn't solve anything. A closet is only a closet, no matter how much you love it. You can be as happy as you want in here, but outside? Nothing. You need to know, Mina. You don't want to turn into Jell-O.

"You might think it's big enough in the closet, but you have to consider what's outside.

"It's so nice and sweet in here. But it's still only a closet. So...tomorrow I'm going to school even though I hate it. I don't want to leave this closet but I will. I swear.

"Ha!" She's overjoyed to have discovered Mina's secret. Armed with this knowledge, chewing on Jell-O, she silently gloats.

That's when it hits her that she no longer loves Mina. The reason love is secret is being secret maintains it. And now that she has Mina's secret in hand she can no longer love her. And that's that—she decides to forget about Mina. Now she can regard her with unadorned contempt. Having erased Mina, she continues to chew Jell-O. As always, what's unnecessary is wiped clean from her memory. Time is still frozen at 9:20 p.m., and in the spacious closet no more words are spoken.

PART TWO

THE OLD PART OF TOWN

It's a hot afternoon when Mina drops in on Crystal.

"What're you up to?" asks Mina with a sheepish grin as she leans against the doorframe. Her fair ankle peeks out between her jeans and sneaker.

Crystal looks at her, arms folded.

"What're you up to?" Mina says again.

Arms still crossed, Crystal says, "Just looking." She has a serious expression.

"Looking at what?"

"You…what else?"

"Let's go out."

"I don't want to."

"Do I care?" Mina takes Crystal by the wrist. Crystal never expected this, and before she knows it she's been led into the corridor. Still holding on to Crystal, Mina pushes the Down button for the elevator. Head down, Crystal scratches her arm. "Did you move or something?"

"No, why?"

"Just wondering. You haven't been stopping by."

"Well, you haven't either."

They take their time jaywalking across the eight-lane

avenue. Cars whiz by them. Powdery gray dust settles on their T-shirts.

"How about some crepes?" says Mina, pointing off into the distance.

"No."

"I'm going to get some anyway."

Blocking the sun with the hand holding her crepe, Mina says, "I need to buy some dark glasses."

Crystal keeps looking at her with a scowl.

"Don't do that," says Mina.

"Why not?"

"You'll get wrinkles."

Erasing the scowl, Crystal gently lowers her head in anticipation of the moment she'll speak up, say what she has to say, and hear the response—but that moment doesn't arrive. Tilting her head slightly, she observes Mina next to her, munching a crepe.

"What's going on with you?" says Crystal. "Taking it easy?"

"No, I'm…" Mina takes another bite of the crepe slathered in honey butter. "…going to school." And with the back of her hand she wipes butter from her mouth.

"Did you transfer?"

"Not to a regular school. An alternative school."

Crystal bursts into laughter. "Wow—way to go, Mina! How do you like it?"

"It's okay." Mina frowns. "The kids are seriously stupid. It's a Hall of Fame of total idiots," she says, spreading her arms wide in emphasis.

"Why am I not surprised."

"Really! A full assortment of idiots, take your pick: love-deprived sickos, losers, misfits, hypochondriacs, kids with personality disorders, kids who are mentally ill, or at least faking it—and that last bunch is so *boring*."

And you're a perfect fit. With this thought Crystal affectionately links arms with Mina. *You're one of them! Am I supposed to be jealous of you?* With an affectionate smile Crystal looks at Mina, who's in her own world as she licks the crepe with her eyes down. No matter how much Crystal looks she just can't figure Mina out...

"Are you still reading that book by the guy who ran the mental hospital?"

"A guy who ran a mental hospital? Which book? Sounds interesting. What's the name of it?"

"Mina...you know what I'm talking about—that book you were reading. There was a doctor a long time ago, he identified a mental illness. I think he wrote the book, but maybe it was his student? Anyway, that's the one. You don't remember?"

"Um, let's see... Jung? Is that who you mean? He ran a mental hospital? Come on, you're making stuff up again."

"Who cares. Anyway, are you still reading it?"

"No. Why are you asking?"

"Is the crepe any good?"

"Yeah. Want some?"

"Nope."

"Let's go to the old part of the city; we can take the bus." Mina tugs on Crystal's arm.

"I don't feel like it. I didn't bring any money or my phone."

"Don't worry, I can pay for both of us."

They hop on the bus and bow, as schoolgirls should, to the driver in his Ray-Ban sunglasses. He has a coppery complexion and his hair is fine and silvered. There are very few passengers. A human interest story about a factory worker streams from the radio. The bus rattles into motion. The air-conditioning chills their pale arms. Taking out her MP3 player, Mina offers one of her headphones to Crystal.

"Who are you listening to?"

"Promise you won't laugh," says Mina, blushing furiously. "Justin Timberlake. Don't laugh."

"What? Are you serious?"

"I said, don't laugh."

"You're going to a school for dumbasses, and the next thing you know you're just like them."

"I don't know. I'm kind of obsessed with him these days."

"How come?"

Mina wishes she could shrink into a cockroach or a cricket and disappear between the seats.

"I can't figure it out either. How can I put it? He's just going through the motions, don't you think? A lightweight. Half-assed singing, half-assed dancing, half-assed flirting. But I think there's more to him. I don't know, he's playful, but to me that somehow gives him some weight." She punctuates her answer with a determined nod, then looks out the window.

"I don't think so."

"You don't think what?"

"He's not playful. He may seem like it to you, because you can't see him any other way. But he's actually doing his best, and he *is* serious."

"What? You like him too? Really? Since when?"

"No way." Crystal scowls. "No. I don't like him. I don't even really know who he is…never seen him."

"Oh stop. Of course you've seen him. He's all over TV, every day."

"Maybe, but I can't remember."

Mina cracks the window and tosses the crepe wrapper

out. It's made of fine plastic, white with tiny silver dots, and Crystal follows its flight, thinking it's beautiful how the brand name is printed in orange all over the wrapper. In no time it has disappeared and Crystal's gaze returns to Mina. The driver yells at Mina. Mina extends her middle finger next to her thigh and giggles. "Dickhead."

"Language, Mina."

"What's the matter?"

"What are people going to think?"

"About what?"

"About you—they'll think you're garbage."

"Shut up."

The light turns red and the bus stops. A banner hangs, fluttering, from a rooftop railing. Mina points at it. It's five stories up, the ivory color barely visible through a layer of crud. The sign says Samik Self-Study Hall.

"That's where she died," Mina says to Crystal, smiling as she says it.

"Who?"

"Chiye."

Crystal smirks.

"Why are you smiling?"

"You smiled first."

"No, I didn't."

"Sure you did—just now."

"No, I didn't. When? When did I do that?"

"All right, you win. Sorry. I guess I was seeing things."

"No…actually…" Mina's face hardens. "You're right—I *was* smiling."

Crystal nods, "It's okay. You can smile. Smile all you want. It's better than crying."

"I'm losing my mind."

"No, you're not. You're normal. Why would you be going crazy?"

"Because I didn't want to smile but I did."

"That's why I like you." Crystal smiles, and Mina does too.

"Why did she do it?" asks Crystal. "Why would she want to kill herself? I just don't get it. Despair? Something like that? What's such a big deal about despair anyway? You won't find me killing myself because of despair, you know that."

Mina doesn't respond.

Crystal sighs. "Lately I feel like throwing crepe wrappers out of windows and killing whoever has the bad luck to get hit by one of them. Or maybe everybody. I just want to kill."

"A gun would make it easy. You could shoot from a distance, spray everyone with bullets."

"Not as easy as you think. Guns are heavy. Besides, everybody's scrambling to get out of the way and bullets are so tiny."

"So you run after them and keep shooting. Hey, we're here, let's get off."

They're in the middle of the old city. They cut beneath a huge overpass, the elevated section of a twelve-lane avenue.

"Let's go that way."

Crystal's eyes follow where Mina's hand points.

They're in a gently winding alley surfaced with square cobbles and bordered by low brick walls capped with red and blue tiles. It's just wide enough for them to squeeze through side by side. A young woman in a black suit holding a gaudy, flower-pattern parasol is coming their way. She stops to let them pass single file. The woman gives off a fragrance of citrus. A cracked vase containing chunks of Styrofoam and a broken-down umbrella sit to one side. A dog barks. A scent of lilac hangs in the air and a magnolia tree comes into sight above the wall. The sky is the brilliant color of a fresh lemon. Underfoot, no two cobbles are level and even. Crystal looks back and sees only a wall; the alley curves out of sight. Beds of lettuce sit on a low rooftop, leaves fluttering in the breeze. The sun has a languid feel and the alley stretches out endlessly in silence. The sun is getting stronger. The two of them trudge along without making a sound, heads down and hands in their pockets. Warm air tickles their cheeks. The sun alternately beats down on their backs and massages their bellies. On they go. Their lungs are heating up. A child is whining. Flushed and languid from the sun, they enter a dreamlike state. The alley is going up now. Crystal and Mina step lightly through the sunlight, their feet leading them steadily toward the sky. But Crystal keeps looking back, her expression fearful. The breeze picks up and the sun changes color. Crystal looks back again: the wall blocks the view of the alley again. She looks at Mina. Eyes half closed, Mina sways along, listening to her headphones. *Dizzy*. Crystal is scared. *Dizzy*. Her head hurts. *Dizzy*. Her head is about to split open. She sees two beetles, locked together as they mate, crawling up the wall, and she starts screaming: "Aaaaaaaaaaa aaaaaaaaauaaaaak let me out of here aaaaaaaa I don't know where I'm uaaauaaa uaaauaaa uaaaaaga…aaa…"

Pushing against the wall as if determined to topple it, Crystal slides writhing onto the cobbles. To Mina it's surreal, a scene from a nightmare. Terrified, she steps back from Crystal, calling out her name at the same time. Crystal's screaming, shrill and yet sleek and lovely, boils over and slowly subsides. Silence returns to the alley. Mina looks around, then gingerly approaches and shakes Crystal's shoulder. Slowly

Crystal looks up, her face bright red. Her forehead is a sheet of perspiration, her irises uncommonly dark. Crystal shuts her eyes tight, then opens them wide and looks up at Mina. Mina can't read Crystal's expression and it makes her uneasy. *Is she angry? Crazy? Sad? Is there such a thing as alley-phobia?*

"Are you all right?"

"Yeah. Sorry about that."

"Don't worry, I'm fine. Let's get out of here. Sorry that happened."

"You don't need to be sorry. But yeah, let's get out of here. I need some air."

Crystal's face is back to its normal color. But where she's holding on to Mina her hand is still warm.

Outside the alley they walk for a while in silence before coming to a crosswalk. Looking to their left, they catch sight of P Bridge. It's part of a four-fold scene—*gray, blue, titanium white,* and *charcoal*; clouds, sky, bridge, and walkway. Slanting shafts of golden sunlight shower down on it.

"Let's take the bridge," says Crystal, pointing in that direction.

Except for the deep red arches, the steel superstructure is white. The walkway is dark gray asphalt and lets out a roar whenever cars pass by. On the far side of the river, against a backdrop of apartment buildings and factory smokestacks, a pleasure boat motors by, its dirty beige froth of wake looking like a mass of hands.

"What's new with you?" Mina ventures.

"What do you want to hear?"

"Whatever you want to tell me."

"Is it okay if I'm not totally up front with you?" Crystal watches Mina. "You're telling me to say whatever I want? Do I have that correct? All right, then, you're hoping I'm not doing well because you're not around—right? But you're wrong—I'm doing just fine."

"Then why are you angry?"

"Who says I'm angry?" Crystal produces a theatrical laugh. "I'm laughing, see? Laughing. So how can I be angry? How's Minho? Is he getting along okay?"

"That dumbass? He broke up with his girlfriend."

"Wow."

"Best news you've heard in a while."

"Did he really? You're serious? Wow, that's great!" Crystal looks up at the sky, putting her hands together. "I'm going to fall in love with him, starting now. I just decided."

"Hey, watch out for that bicycle."

Crystal looks down with wide eyes. There's no bicycle. She glowers at Mina and Mina responds with a grin.

"Congrats! You're weirder than ever."

"Liar. You're the one who's weird… How's the new school, really? You're okay there?"

"I told you, I don't want to talk about it. I didn't want to go but my mom made me—she said I'd be all right, that one of her friends teaches there. Shit. I can't believe I fell for that."

"So, are you all right there?"

"Well, since they say it's all right, I guess it's all right… sure it's all right. Fuck—what am I saying? The kids all think they're so ridiculously special. They're so starved for attention, all they do is fixate on how to make themselves stand out. You know, shaved heads, mismatched socks. Just for the attention! If they really want to dress weird, if that's what they want, what they really want, then of course I can understand. But if not? One glance tells me if it's to get attention or if it's really what the kid wants. One glance says it all. To me, to you, whoever. And it's all about attention, finding out what the other kids think, it's what's on their minds all day long. The difference is that instead of wanting to look a little more normal they want to look a little less normal. But the bottom line's the same, isn't it? It's so *boring*. They all think they're so special. I just wish I could clue them in, tell them to their faces."

"Why don't you?"

"Yeah, maybe I should. But I feel kind of sorry for them, you know? But on the other hand… There's this kid who writes poetry. I had a look at it and it's garbage. But the teachers *rave* about it. What the fuck? It really pisses me off. At least the kids in our school didn't write poetry. But *these* kids are, like, straight out of the eighteenth century, from some no-name place on the border of Europe before capitalism, Catholics who made a living by milking goats."

"Hard to imagine."

"Seriously. I had no clue before I got there—I never would have believed kids like this exist. And the teachers? They're like Buddha bobble-heads. It's totally messed up!"

"Then why did you transfer? I just don't get it."

Mina pauses and looks at Crystal. "I was having nightmares. Every night. They made me not want to go to sleep. It turned into insomnia." Mina's face is red. "I wish I could forget those dreams but I can't."

"Mina, please don't cry."

"I'm not crying, bitch… My mom told me she called Dad and said she was afraid I was going to kill myself. She was crying."

"So, were you?"

"No—why would I want to do that! There's so much that people don't get about me! Shit! Mom said that if school was taking so much out of me, then I shouldn't go. But was that the problem? Was it really the school? For sure? Who knows?

I mean, maybe it was. I don't know. It got to the point where I didn't know what was what. And then… And then… In the end I just accepted it. Just accepted it. I wanted to sleep. *Really* sleep. But I couldn't. And so… And so… And so… what? Oh hell, what am I saying?"

"I don't know."

"Me neither."

"Ah, I like how the river smells."

"Not me."

"Anyway, don't get on Minho's case. He's mine now."

"What! You must think I'm nuts or something. Anyway, I thought you had a boyfriend. Did you break up with him already?"

"No, he's still around. But he's him and Minho's Minho."

"That's pathetic!"

"What is?"

"You."

A woman on crutches with her leg in a cast approaches them. They back away from each other to make way for her. She's followed by two bicycles and a jogger, and now the two girls are farther apart.

"You still live in the same place?" asks Crystal, closing the gap. "You didn't move, did you?"

"Huh? Um, uh, no, I didn't. I already told you that. You don't believe me?"

"Why do I have this feeling you moved? Anyway…you know…I killed a kitten the other day."

"What? How come?"

Crystal scowls, and in the next moment is pressing down with her left hand on the fingertips of her right hand.

"Why're you doing that? Something wrong with your hands?"

Crystal shakes her head. "Doing anything tomorrow?"

"Let's see, after school…nothing much. I'll be done at one."

"Great, then let's meet tomorrow. We'll go somewhere."

"What about you? Don't you have school? And cram school? And tutoring?"

"Tomorrow's a holiday, the school's anniversary—you forgot already? I don't have tutoring tomorrow, and I'll call in sick for cram school."

"Who besides you would remember the school anniversary?"

"Out of sight, out of mind—good for you. Me, I remember everything."

Silent again, the two girls start across the bridge. Looking up, they see dark gray clouds shrouding the bridge towers. Looking back down, they make their way under the clouds, still not talking. The bridge feels as if it's inching upward toward the sky and then, just as gradually, it drops down. A woman wearing a black cap, mask, and gloves jogs past with a huge dog in tow. A group of boys pass by them on bikes, full of vitality. At the far end of the bridge the bus stop comes into view, and then the bus. They set off running for it.

The bus makes its sluggish way out of the old part of the city. The sidewalks are swarming with tourists in backpacks and women window-shopping, and the narrow, winding, crisscrossing alleys are choked and smoggy with cars. The entire area from beneath the ground to the hilltops is crowded with places for people to live. In contrast, the newer part of the city, the suburb where Crystal and Mina live, was planned, laid out in a grid on the flat land—a crush of perfectly squared box-shaped cement buildings and streets that stretch out freely and easily among them, giving off a buzz of energy. A practical combination of lines and surfaces.

While the cramped riot of streets gives way to wide, straight, simple avenues, the sun gradually sets. The avenues stretch out, perfectly plumb and endless. Every few minutes they see commercial establishments with identical signs and interior design: a pizza parlor, bakery, and steak house, then a different bakery, cheesecake shop, and coffee shop, and then a different coffee shop, salad buffet place, and Vietnamese restaurant, every one of them a company franchise. The swaying bus lurches to a stop at yet another store packed with merchandise. The faces of the two girls remain peaceful, compressed by a lifetime of repeated experiences in the forty minutes they've been on the bus. Crystal thinks about the alley from earlier in the day; Mina, the Samik Self-Study Hall. Mina thinks about Crystal's screaming; Crystal feels drowsy. Thanking the driver in chirpy voices, they hop off the bus at a boundary where there are fewer cars and buildings and the background changes from gray to dark green. The scenery is pleasant in its simplicity, the air pungent with the smell of grass. Crystal boards a different bus as Mina waves goodbye. Crystal waves back. The bus takes off and Mina slowly crosses the street, disappearing down a well-tended walking path. Past the path the bus turns right and the next moment Mina can no longer see it.

PARTY TIME

Dressed in a black tracksuit with a large black backpack on, Crystal sets out for Mina's place. When she arrives, the door opens and the champagne-colored chandelier in the living room shines dreamily, with five layers of candle-like bulbs and, suspended evenly beneath them, large turquoise stones and delicately cut crystal in the form of water droplets. As she always does, she counts the bulbs and nods. Twelve of them, all present and accounted for.

Mina emerges from her room, pencil and a workbook of practice problems for the high school equivalency exam in hand. She's wearing a T-shirt and cutoffs and her hair is gathered back in a ponytail.

"Where's Minho?"

"He's not back from school yet."

"Oh?"

"Is that why you're here?"

"Your place hasn't changed at all."

"Meaning?"

"Does Minho have cram school tonight?"

"I'm not sure. What's with the backpack?"

"Oh, just stuff."

"What stuff?"

"Strawberries."

"Strawberries?"

Crystal unzips her backpack and takes out a Ziploc bag full of strawberries.

"Somebody gave them to my mom. She said we need to eat them before they go bad. We could maybe make jam out of them?"

"I don't know how."

"Me neither."

"That's it?"

"That's it."

"Really. You had me worried there for a moment."

"Like I had something else?"

"Workbooks, maybe?"

"Have we ever studied together?"

"Nope."

"How about some music, Mina?"

"What do you want to hear?"

"Something fun. How about…New Order?"

"Don't have anything of theirs."

"That sucks."

"Minho's got them on his laptop."

Crystal sets down her backpack. Mina takes the bag of strawberries to the dining table.

Crystal hooks Minho's laptop up to the speakers. "Come on, Minho…where are you, Minho…when're you going to get here, Minho, and watch a movie with us?"

"Stop mumbling and let's have a drink."

"What have you got?"

"Vodka."

Mina fetches a bottle of SKYY Vodka and a bottle of

cranberry juice and gives Crystal a wink.

"Cool. But won't you catch hell from your mom when she finds out?"

"She won't be home tonight."

"How come?"

"She's away on a business trip. And when has she ever said anything about you and me drinking?"

"We get an earful if she sees us smoking."

"That's just because she wants to smoke too."

"Let's call Minho, tell him to get his butt home so we can all have a drink together."

"Go ahead."

"Huh?"

"He's got a life of his own, you know. Besides, he's not too crazy about hanging out with us."

"Liar. You can't be serious? Really? I don't believe you. Liar."

"No lie, it's the truth."

"Still…even so…Mina, call him anyway. Get him over here. Come on, Mina."

"All right. Hold on." Mina sends him a text. "Done."

"No answer? Mina, tell him to hurry it up."

"Bitch, it's only been three seconds."

Crystal looks at Mina with a morose expression. It makes her look like a motherless puppy that people would want to go up to and pet. Mina goes over to her. Crystal continues to watch her. What's Mina to do? She keeps telling herself Crystal isn't a puppy. But she ends up petting her anyway.

"*What* are you doing?"

"Your hair's all messed up."

"Really? Oh, then thanks."

The song ends and somehow it feels chilly. Standing still,

the two of them wait for the next song, but it doesn't come. Mina walks over to the laptop and hits the repeat button. She turns around and flinches—Crystal's right behind her.

"What's the problem, you having a heart attack or something?"

"I thought you were a ghost."

Crystal giggles. "Mina, tell me—you feeling okay? Still depressed?"

Silence.

"Are you having a hard time? You still feel like killing yourself?"

Instead of answering, Mina scurries to the TV. Crystal follows her and pats her on the shoulder. "What's wrong? You can tell me…okay, if you don't want to, that's fine."

"What is it you want to hear?"

"Whatever you want to tell me."

Mina smiles. "All right, at this moment, right now, I really don't like you."

Crystal looks flustered. "I'm sorry if I made you angry. I wish I knew why I always make you that way…"

"You want to."

"Why would I want *that*?"

"You want me angry."

"But why?"

"You're asking me? How should I know!"

"Mina, settle down. You know…"

"What?"

"What kind of person do you think I am?"

"I don't get it."

"What I mean…" Crystal looks at Mina. For the briefest moment Mina's face frosts over, but Crystal misses it. "What I mean is…I wanted to say I'm sorry. I wanted to have a heart-to-heart with you but I guess it didn't happen. Sorry."

Silence.

"I'm sorry I couldn't help you."

"Crystal, don't, please, not now."

Crystal's face crumbles.

She wants to have a serious talk with Mina. She wants Mina to throw herself open in front of her like before, sobbing about how she wants to kill herself. Then she'd surely open up to Mina and there they'd be, heart to heart. But there's no pungent scent of pine needles now, no more giddy sunlight. Crystal has already rejected Mina, which means Mina will never open up to her again. Crystal has lost the chance to get close to Mina. She can't turn the clock back, can't put together what's been broken. *Well, who cares?*

"I hope you're all right. But really, it's not like you weren't all right before." Crystal lays out her new hypothesis: "We were closer then, because Chiye was gone. I was the only one who was really there for you. But it didn't work out. I wasn't nice to you, that's why. I should have said it before, but I'm sorry I wasn't nice to you. And from now on I'd like us to be closer."

"As for me…"

"As for you?"

"I'm thinking it's too late."

Crystal opens her arms to Mina. "I…"

"It's too late."

"I…I…" She gesticulates, her arms flared. "I…I…I…"

"Hey, Crystal…"

"I…I…I…I…I…I…I…"

"Crystal, come on…"

"I…oh hell…" Crystal drops her arms and glares at Mina. There's a look in her eye that Mina can't read. "So, it's because of that?"

"What do you mean?"

"Nothing else to ask me? Nothing you've been wondering about?"

"Ask you about what?"

"Me screaming in the alley yesterday, me killing a kitten, what else—does there have to be something else? Don't act like you don't know. What's wrong? You're faking, aren't you? But why? Mina…look—don't *do* that. Don't. I need your attention." She takes Mina's hands and shakes them, Mina's arms jostling listlessly in turn. "Why aren't you answering, why don't you answer? Answer me, say something!"

"Stop it. You're making me dizzy."

"Sorry." Crystal lets go of her.

"You've always been like this."

"Like what?"

"Flying off the handle and screaming for no reason, out of the blue. You know that. You've scared me so many times, but I've gotten used to it."

"Liar. You're still jumpy."

"Look…"

"When have I ever done that? When?"

"All the time. That's why I'm so scared of you! And I don't mean sometimes or even most of the time, I mean *always*."

"So why didn't you say it?"

"Say what?"

Crystal spreads her arms wide to demonstrate. "Something like this."

"Meaning what?"

"An expression. *I'm so scared*. Something like that. An expression." Crystal's face is serious. But Mina giggles.

"What's so funny?"

"You look like a comedian."

"Well, I'm not."

"All right, that's enough."

"Enough of what?"

"Okay, let's suppose I did that, I *expressed* myself. Then what? I say something and you'd change somehow? But you're always the same. The same girl. You'll never change, I know it. Always the same. You're just a scary kid. When you told me you killed a kitten it was shocking, I'll admit it. But I wasn't actually all that surprised. Because you're the sort of person who could kill a kitten. Based on the years I've known you I think it's safe to say that. You're the sort of person who could kill a kitten. It wasn't even that hard for you, was it? No, it was easy. And there's something else. What you say never adds up. Actually I shouldn't say that…it *does* add up, but only from your point of view. You laugh when you cry. You scream your head off while you laugh. And has there ever been a time when you really, truly paid attention to me? How about when I was having nightmares?" Mina chokes up. "Or when things were so hard I thought about killing myself? What did you do? Tell me. *Cheesecake.* You wanted some cheesecake, remember?"

"I'm sorry, Mina, really I am." Sheepishly Crystal points to her belly. "I was starved, that's why."

"Look at you. This is exactly what I mean." Mina wipes her teary eyes with the back of her hand.

"Don't cry, Mina." Crystal reaches out to her.

"No!" screams Mina. "Don't touch me!" She jumps to her feet. "You don't treat me as an equal. You don't treat *anyone* as your equal. You line us all up and keep us under your thumb. I've always known, from the very beginning. I could see it from the look in your eyes. One look at you and anyone could tell.

We just don't say it to your face. Why should we bother? Who needs the annoyance? And it's not like you'd care. Anyway, I've always known. But I kept hanging out with you. Because you're fun. You're a fun person and fun to hang out with. And because you had fun hanging out with me. But the point is, none of that matters. To be honest, I'll never understand the way you think—this person's worthy, that person's unworthy. I don't get it, but I've lost interest trying to. I don't care if you line up people or build them into a pyramid. It's draining. But just because I don't want to be bothered anymore doesn't mean I don't know anything about you. I do, to an extent. You're capable of killing a kitten just because it didn't obey you and you got mad. I can tell. You're like a kid, so, like a kid, you can be unpredictable. You scare me. Everybody's like you, or else they want to be. That why I'm scared. Scared to death. In fact, I probably died. I died already. I'm sick of this life. It's not normal. Cram school, home, school, test, school, cram school, homework, tutor, cram school, home, tutor, cram school, home, school, back to cram school, back to tutor, back for a test back to homework back to school back to school back to school. Home. Cram school. How can anyone think this is normal? It's crazy. Everyone's crazy. I can't stand it. Not anymore! I can't stand this life. This is hell. It's hell. Hell Chosŏn! Our society is hell! That's why Chiye killed herself. I get it. But you don't, do you? I can understand it, and that's the difference between you and me. It's because of people like you that Chiye killed herself. You're a killer. But you don't know it. Never will. Not in your lifetime. I know what kids like you are like. I didn't before but I do now. To me it's like you're not even a living thing, it's like you're inanimate. You're more like that sofa than you are like me. But how is that possible? I'll never understand it. I'll never truly understand *you*.

I know—I know what you think of me. You look down on me. But do I care? All that stuff is meaningless. Just keep your eyes straight ahead, I tell myself, and as long as I do that I'll be all right, no matter what anybody else does. But honestly, you treat me like an idiot and every now and then I get mad. And I'm sick of it. I hate it. But that's over now. I'm over all that."

"So I guess you don't like me."

"Let's talk about something else."

"Sure, but first I need a recap. What you're saying is that you're better than me, that I treat you like shit but I'm wrong. You're saying that *you're* the one who's better, *you're* the one who looks down on *me*. Did I get that right?"

"What the hell has short-circuited in your brain? How in hell can you put those twisted words in my mouth? It's *amazing*. How many times do I have to say it? I *told* you, I don't have the slightest interest in your who's-better, who's-worse thinking! I'm not concerned whether you look up, down, or sideways at people! But that doesn't mean I don't know anything! The point is, I just don't want to be bothered. *That's* what I said. Got it?"

"Hey, but let's be honest. You can *afford* not to be interested, right? That's you. You have a wonderful life. Nothing missing, everything peaceful and easy."

"What about you? Why are you so needy; what's stopping you from having a wonderful life? You're smarter than me. Better off. Better-looking. You're a better person than I am, much better. And I know how intelligent you are."

"No, you're smarter. You read Freud and Jung and listen to more music than I do."

"Nope, you're still smarter. I checked out those books as a joke. To be honest, I didn't understand a word of it, really.

Maybe I was just trying to look cool. You know that I like to try and be cool, don't you?"

"Come on, cut the shit, Mina. You're smart. Smarter than me. I know that. You just don't try. You poured yourself into *Jung*," Crystal says with outstretched arms, "but not your schoolwork."

"I didn't get to page thirty of Jung."

"Oh? Well, um… The others, then, let's see. Who were the other authors you were reading? That guy who tutored us, you knew all the books he mentioned. I didn't but you did. You knew Deleuze, you knew Derrida…who else? Oh yeah, Marx. You knew all of them."

"You know Marx."

"Your family is richer than mine, too."

Mina looks at her. Whatever she was going to say next is lost.

"Cat got your tongue, Mina?"

"Hey—who *are* you? Who are you anyway? *What* are you? What kind of person are you? I've always known you had a weird side. Very weird. But now I see you're weird to the bone."

"And you're *rich* to the bone. You're from such a rich family. Not me. You have everything. Not me."

"What more do I have than you?"

"Listen to Little Miss Innocent! You're not making sense, Mina. *Everybody* knows your family's better off than mine. Why are you playing dumb? It's *preposterous*! Look around you, this is where you *live*. La-di-da!"

"Fuck! All right, let's suppose this place is bigger than yours, and we have more money than you…"

"Suppose? Those aren't suppositions, they're *facts*."

"All right, facts. Fuck it! All right, so we're filthy rich! Are you happy now? Why are we talking about this? Why am *I* talking about this? You are really fucking annoying. All right, suppose we're rich. Shit…what am I trying to say? Okay. Okay, here's the thing. Why do you have this victim's mentality? Yeah, that's it. Or is it? Look…. Oh hell… You made me forget what I was going to say. You and your… Fuck!… Okay, I got it. Now I remember. Okay…. You're smarter than me. Your family may not be as rich as mine, *but*—the fact is, we're not rich. We're so far in debt it's not funny. I really feel sorry for my mom. Fuck—why am I telling you any of this? This is so annoying and it's all your fault. Would you *please* stop making that face, I *hate* you when you do that. So guess what? We're the only ones in this building that don't have foreign cars. We got rich suddenly, right? So people talk about us behind our backs, though they would never say anything directly to us. Have I told you how we used to live? Not dirt poor, but poor. Every month we worried about getting by. We still worry. When I was a kid I used to buy clothes at the street market. One time I was at the market with my mom and I wanted some kimchi dumplings so fucking bad but my mom didn't have any money and she wouldn't buy them for me and I started bawling and I got a fucking beating. Anything like that ever happen to you? No, of course not. When you get right down to it, your family has a better life than mine—all things being equal. Ask yourself: 'Is there anything I can't do because I can't afford it?' The answer's no, correct? Anyway, you're an only child, so Mom and Dad give you everything. But me, I have to split things with Minho, and he gets twice as much as I do, because he's the only son of an only son. As if that makes him precious. Isn't that *preposterous*? It's not like he's the only son of an only son of an only son. But that's not an issue for you. And you get good grades. And you're good at scoring boyfriends. So what's your problem? I know what you think of me, I can see it in your eyes. You feel so sorry for yourself every day. You don't want to invite me over to your place. Instead you come here and drool over that ugly-ass chandelier, the park, the fountain, the parking lot full of fancy foreign cars. What's the matter with you? Aren't there plenty of foreign cars in the parking lot of your building? I *totally* don't get it. I'm no match for you grades-wise. But you're always sneaking looks at my grades anyway. You read my writing assignments but never let me read yours…"

"I'm sorry, but I think the chandelier is pretty."

"Look, this conversation is *not* about 'Let's make Crystal feel bad.' You don't have to apologize for anything. It's just that I'll never understand you. Why do you get so anxious, why so pissed off? Why so scared? Why are you always so jumpy, as if you're standing on needles? Why do you look at me with your eyes full of poison? Crystal, you give me the creeps. Sometimes I watch you and wonder why you're always trying to get on top of everyone else; it's like people are walking all over you and you need to get even—I just don't get it. Are you the brave little elevator, or what? And the *kitten*. Why'd you kill it? You really did kill a kitten, right? And so? Don't bother saying anything…I think I've got a pretty good idea. You'll say you killed it because you were afraid. Does that make sense? You were scared so you killed it? You think you're so special that fear gives you the power of life or death over anyone and anything?"

"No! That's not it! You're wrong! We were just playing around, grabbing each other, it was an accident that it died. And the truth is…no…I don't know why I killed it. I'm trying not to think about it. I don't think I'll ever know the reason. Or if I do, it'll scare me, you know? Scare me to death. Why would I kill a kitten? I'm afraid to know. I'm awful, I know that. And I regret it."

"That's what you always say."

"No, I mean it. Mina, believe me. I even had a dream about it. So I..." Instead of finishing the sentence Crystal walks over to Mina and takes her by the hands.

"Don't do that, please. You scare me when you hold my hands and smile like that."

"Really?"

"So what were you about to say?'

"I ended up going into my closet."

"And?"

"What do you mean, 'And?' You like to go into your closet. I thought you'd be happy to know I went into mine."

"You're really losing it."

"What do you mean? You don't go into your closet anymore?"

"Sure I do."

"Then what's the point?"

"What does me going into my closet have to do with you? You went into your closet just because I go into mine? But why? Fine—your call. But why should I be happy knowing you went in your closet? That's so crazy!"

"Hey—"

"Wait, Minho just texted."

"And?"

"He'll be back by four. But he says he's tired."

"Who cares. What time is it?"

"Two thirty."

"Fine. More time for us to bitch at each other. Where were we?"

"Closets."

"Right, closets. So…" Crystal nods, then covers her smile with her hand like a little girl. "Know what? I figured out your secret! For real."

"What secret?"

"What you do in your closet."

"And what do I do in my closet?"

"Jell-O."

"Jell-O?"

"You've been eating Jell-O in your closet. And you never wanted to come out, right? Fess up!"

"Crystal?"

"Hmm?"

"Did it ever occur to you that you drain all the energy out of me?"

Mouth shut and pride wounded, Crystal looks at Mina.

"I mean—"

"Okay…. Right. Got it. Let's take a break. I'm tired too. So what do we do now? Clean?"

"Our place is always clean anyway."

"Yeah, you're right. Then let's make a cake with those strawberries."

"Whatever you say."

Shoulders drooping, they go into the kitchen, dump the bag of strawberries in the sink, and stand side by side rinsing the berries. An awkward silence lingers.

"You know how to make a strawberry cake?" Mina asks.

"Nope. What about you?"

"Me neither. Hey, did you bring any smokes?"

"Can we? Is it okay?"

"Just for today. But only on the balcony. Come on." They leave the kitchen together, pass through the dining room, and from the living room go out onto the balcony.

Crystal takes a pack of cigarettes from her pants pocket. "Here you go."

"I have some too."

"Cool."

"Can I use your lighter?" Mina lights her own cigarette and then Crystal's, saying, "Wow, this is to die for, especially today."

"Thanks."

"Sure. And thanks to Mr. Philip Morris for giving us the opportunity to get hooked on cigarettes."

"You got such a great view!"

"Of what?"

"Look, right there in front of you. From up here, don't you feel like you're the master of everything you see? Like it's all yours. Though I guess there are lots people who can look out on the city from this angle. And they probably think the same thing."

"You're the only one."

"Really?"

"Uh, by the way…"

"Hmm?"

"Oh, never mind."

"No, tell me, Mina."

"No, it's nothing. So, are we done talking? We're done. We're done now, right?"

"Mm-hmm." Crystal nods. "What did we talk about anyway?"

"Oh, I don't know. I don't want to think about it anymore. It's annoying."

"Me neither."

"And that's why you and I just don't click. We get on each other's nerves. I'm going in."

"No. Stay."

"Fuck this! What are we doing anyway? All this really pisses me off. And I was already really pissed off before. As we fought about who's smarter, deep down I was thinking: what the fuck are we doing, this is really, totally stupid."

"So why didn't you laugh?"

"How could I? We were both so dead serious."

"I don't know about *that*. What can we do now to make ourselves laugh?"

Crystal and Mina get Minho's laptop and go on Naver.com to find the easiest cake recipe. The berries have bumps but are fresh and the whipped cream is lumpy but tasty. They nibble at their cake with teaspoons while chain-smoking, drinking vodka with cranberry juice, and listening to music. They turn up the volume and lie on the floor, feeling the beat massage their bodies. For the soft, calming songs they lie on the floor, arms swaying, and for the upbeat songs they jump on the sofa, shimmying. They step lightly from one end of the hall to the other, turn in circles, eyes closed, and back in the living room they feel like they're walking on air. Bodies tuned in to the rhythm, they mumble the dirty lyrics but wail the clean ones. For a moment, they are happy and having fun. They're all in. It's a beautiful state of mind and they trust in the fever. The music gets their hearts beating, makes their cheeks rosy, sets their heads bobbing—all of it generating sweet hormones. And this is how Crystal and Mina make up—everything's peachy and they're friends again, as close as ever. But then it's after seven and Minho isn't back yet. Mina's already asleep on the floor. Crystal feels tired—dizzy and languid. She tries to stay awake but sleep is washing over her. She prods Mina. Mina's talking in her sleep. Crystal crushes out her cigarette, finishes her drink, lies down next to Mina, and closes her eyes.

When Minho finally returns, the apartment is thick with stale air and the two girls are sprawled on the floor. On the dining room table is a misshapen slice of strawberry cream cake and a shiny blue bottle. Minho finds a large blanket and covers the girls from head to toe. He takes a strawberry from the leftover pile and pops it into his mouth, then sticks out his tongue and makes a face.

"What's going on?" Minho eases close to Mina and prods her in the side with his foot. Mina squirms once and turns over. Minho smiles, satisfied.

Crystal wakes up and goes to find Minho playing a video game in his room.

She looks over his shoulder at the monitor. "What're you doing?"

He shrugs, and drinks from the carton of milk on his desk.

"I saw you in my dream, *Oppa*."

"What was the dream about?"

"I was leaving for some country or other and you were sending me off. To make my parents happy we went to a Korean restaurant, but you didn't touch a thing. So later we left the airport to find a stir-fried rice cake place. They were everywhere. But the one we found also had king-size squid hung on a line and if you got the squid you got served first."

"Uh-huh."

"But you didn't want squid either, *Oppa*. You didn't want anything. I thought I was going to starve to death."

"What's with the *oppa* all of a sudden?"

"You don't like it?"

"No."

"Well you *should*."

"No."

"Hey!" Suddenly Mina stomps up behind them. "Why're you hitting on my brother? That's gross."

"You said he broke up with his girlfriend."

"But *you* didn't break up with *your* boyfriend…"

"What? Mina," Crystal says, "don't you have anything better to do?"

"You retard, can't you see she's hitting on you? She's already got a guy. Don't say I didn't warn you. And don't come crying to me later."

"Shut up," Minho says. "I've had enough, Mina. Get lost."

"Oh yeah, I'm the one who has to get lost, not Crystal. Okay, have fun, you two. Fuck yourselves to death for all I care."

Mina starts to close the door on them, and, almost by reflex, Crystal tries to keep it open.

"Fuck! Get lost, both of you."

"What's wrong?" Crystal says to Minho.

"I'll leave you two to yourselves," says Mina.

"Hey, Mina, can we *please* stop?"

"Just let me shut the fucking door, will you?"

"Mina," says Minho, "will you *please* back off?"

"Shut up," Mina replies. "Don't I get to have some fun?"

"You call this fun?!" Crystal screams. "What a pain in the ass!"

"You're going to break the door!" shouts Minho.

"No way!" shouts Crystal. "You're not closing this fucking door!"

"Fuck, that's it." Minho gets up and yanks the door open, sending Mina sprawling onto the floor.

Mina shrieks and the next moment bursts out crying, "Asshole—why did you do that to me? You fucking idiot."

Crystal carefully approaches. "You okay?"

Milk carton in hand, Minho slowly comes over as well. "You okay?"

"Fucking idiots, how can I be okay?" Mina glowers at them with teary eyes, her face flushed. "My butt! My butt hurts."

"I didn't pull that hard."

"Sure you didn't, you fucking asshole."

"Mina," says Crystal, placing a hand on her shoulder. "Mina, calm down."

Mina glares at her. "Get your hands off me."

Crystal stares back at Mina. "I'm not the one who did it."

"So?"

"I'm not."

"So what?"

"I didn't do it, I didn't!"

"Will you two *please* stop bitching? That's enough, Mina. It's my fault, I'm sorry."

"Get lost, Minho. You too, Crystal. This is so fucking irritating. Get lost, both of you."

Crystal gives Mina a blank look, then nods abruptly. "All right." She gets her backpack from the dining room and puts it on. "Bye. Take care." Then she snatches the milk carton from Minho and pours milk in a circle around Mina. Lukewarm milk splashes Mina's thigh. "Okay, round and round—that better? Once more, round and round—is that better now? You're all cured. Get up and walk. Get up. Come on…rise. No? Okay, fine. No problem."

In her black tracksuit and black backpack she looks like a farmer spraying herbicide as she continues sprinkling milk on the rose-colored marble floor. After the carton's empty she begins chanting, circling a few more times around Mina. There's milk on Mina's magenta socks and the rose floor. Crystal's chanting reaches the chandelier and the windows, filling the living room, as Minho and Mina follow her movements with rapt gazes. Crystal ends with a huge half circle around Mina, then heads for the door. "Bye—this time for real!"

The door closes, the soothing warble sounds as it locks, and its colorful display briefly lights up.

Minho and Mina look at each other.

"What the hell?" Mina looks at the small puddles of milk. "That fucking bitch! Made a mess and just took off."

"Why don't you go after her?" asks Minho.

"What for?"

"You're going to just let her go?"

"What else can we do?"

"Well for one thing you can go find her. She's acting really weird."

"So, what's new? She's always like that. Totally weird. And look, I'm all wet. How can I go out with my ass soaked?"

Minho scowls at her.

"Then *you* go!"

"I've already decided to." Minho puts on his shoes. "Clean up." The door shuts behind him.

"No way!" Lying on the floor all by herself, Mina calls out Crystal's name, once, twice, and then a third time. The milk, cold, is in her hair, which sticks to the cool marble floor.

Minho bypasses the elevator, opens the emergency exit door, and runs down the stairs. Reaching the ground level, he opens the door and sees the milk carton in Crystal's hand in the last of the sunlight. She's walking, absolutely leisurely, out of the complex. Minho calls her name twice, loudly, then sprints after her. Crystal continues her casual stroll. Minho catches up and falls in beside her, panting. Gathering his breath, he taps her on the shoulder, disposes of the milk carton for her, and returns to her side. Surprised and wary, she looks at him with tearful eyes. Watching her blink, Minho goes blank. He says nothing.

Crystal removes her headphones. "Why are you following me?" she says, wiping her tears with the back of her hand. "Because of Mina?"

"No. Are you heading home?"

Crystal nods, face drooping. She looks like a little birdie that's lost its mother. Seeing her in this state, Minho tries to hold on to his aloofness by recalling how she sprinkled milk around Mina. He's not sure what to say to her, so he simply offers to walk her home. "Let's go."

Crystal hesitates then says okay.

As they walk they keep just enough distance between them to avoid touching. Now and then she looks at him and sees the play of the afterglow on his fair cheeks and lips. Minho senses her gaze but keeps his eyes focused ahead of him. Occasionally he looks off to the side opposite Crystal and scans what's over there, but doesn't register anything, and then he looks straight ahead again. Crystal looks at him. This time she holds the stare, intensifies it. Just as she's about to bump into a telephone pole Minho grabs her by the shoulder.

"Hey, what are you doing? What's the matter?"

"You were about to walk into that pole."

"Oh, thanks."

They resume walking, this time with twice the distance between them, a distance that sometimes contracts by half, sometimes expands by half.

"Um, tell me—do I smell like booze?"

"Nope. Just cigarettes."

"Oh fuck…. What am I going to do?…"

"Wash your hair when you get home."

"You know," she says, looking down at the ground, "you know…I was going to sleep over at your place. So I packed my PJs—and my toothbrush and lotion."

Minho looks at her. With her face down she rubs her nose with the back of her hand—another of her nervous tics—then looks up at Minho. Again he thinks of how she circled Mina, sprinkling the milk.

"There's always next time."

"When? She doesn't want to hang out with me anymore. Right? What am I going to do?"

"No, she'll still hang out with you. She's not really mad."

"I'm pretty sure she won't."

"Yes, she will."

"How do you know?"

"You're her only friend. You know that."

"Yeah, right! She'd rather be by herself than hang out with me. And Mina's the only one who ever hung out with me."

The image of Crystal pouring milk is fixed in Minho's mind—the image has captured him. But he doesn't mention it. And so their conversation stops. They walk in silence. What they see as they follow the streets is mundane, perhaps mirroring their state of mind. Crystal's apartment complex comes into view in the distance. There's something about it that's incomparably barren, something impossible even to symbolize, perhaps mirroring their feelings. At the door to her building Crystal punches the entry code into the number pad and she and Minho enter side by side. Waiting for the elevator, Crystal looks Minho up and down. Seeing his spotless sneakers, she thinks about her own outfit and decides she looks like a member of a third-rate handball club from a rural public school on their way to a training camp at Kyeryong Mountain.

The elevator arrives and they get on together.

"Where are you going?"

"Your place—isn't that where you're going?"

"Yes. But what about you? You want to go to my place too?"

"Is that all right?"

Her heart starts pounding. She looks at him again.

"What for?"

Minho doesn't respond. There's only the hum of the elevator. It comes to a stop and side by side they exit, then enter her apartment.

"Come in, but my room's off-limits." She crosses her arms. "Too messy…" She heads for her room and Minho follows her.

"What do you mean, messy? It's cleaner than Mina's room."

Crystal dramatically squawks in displeasure.

She unzips her black hooded top and peels it off to reveal a pink T-shirt with Dumbo the Flying Elephant. Seeing it, Minho looks surprised. Crystal returns to the living room, perches on the edge of the sofa, and with one hand picks up the phone while with the other she turns on the TV with the remote.

"Mom? Mm-hmm. Just got home. At Mina's. What about you? Busy? Got it. No. All right. When're you coming home? What? And Dad? I ate already. Mm-hmm, at Mina's. I know. Yeah, I've got school tomorrow. Mm-hmm. Right, tomorrow there's school. Yeah, everything's fine. What was that? No. That's ridiculous. Oh, next week I've got to pay the

cram school fee. Right. I know. Okay…yeah…yeah. Bye."
Hanging up, she says, "Want something to drink?"

"Water?"

"Hey, what're you doing in there?" She jumps up and runs to her room. Minho is stretched out on her bed with a smile on his face.

"I don't wash my feet before I go to bed, you know."

Scratching his head, Minho laughs. "And I didn't wash my hair today."

She turns and walks out. Minho follows her. She hands him a small bottle of spring water from the refrigerator.

"When're your parents coming home?"

"They aren't."

"Really?"

"Well…I don't know. Not till late."

"Okay to smoke inside?"

"Umm…no. Out on the balcony. I didn't know you smoked."

Minho takes a pack of cigarettes from his pocket. Unopened. Lucky Strikes.

"Hey, nice. Where'd you get them?"

"From a friend—he got them in Japan."

"Ever tried them? How are they? Any good?"

"First time. Want one?"

She nods. They slide open the glass door, go out, and close it behind them. She opens the outer window wide and the wind rushes in and musses her hair. Minho reaches out and smooths it down.

Crystal scowls. "What are you doing? Does it look funny?"

Instead of answering he lights a cigarette and points at the two metal chairs with silver finish. "Okay to sit?"

"Not okay."

"Fine."

"Just kidding. Go ahead, sit. That's what they're there for. They're called chairs."

"Yeah, I can see that."

Crystal lowers her head and giggles.

"What's so funny?"

"You are."

"Stop laughing and sit down." Minho pulls on her arm and she plops into the chair next to him. She turns and sees his face a hand-length away.

"*Oppa*, is it true you broke up with your girlfriend?"

"Let's not talk about that."

"Why'd you break up with her?"

"Just because. I don't know." For a time he's lost in thought. "It was me. I was the one who suggested it."

"And she went along with it?"

"What?"

"What did she *say*?"

"I don't know. We stopped calling each other."

"She stopped calling you? How come?"

"No, it was me."

"How come?"

"I told you I don't want to talk about it." He pulls at his hair. Crystal's eyes narrow to slits. "Like I said, I didn't wash my hair today and it's driving me nuts it's so itchy. Just kidding. I did wash it. This morning. She keeps calling me."

"And?"

"Well…" With a shrug Minho says, "I leave my cell-phone off."

"Bad boy." With her hands she neatens his messed-up hair. "My boyfriend's a good guy."

"That's nice."

"Mmm."

"Where do I get rid of this?"

She points to a large metal plate on the floor beneath the chairs.

"Wow, that's an ashtray? Cool."

"Obviously not."

"How long you been with him?"

"Oh…maybe four weeks?"

"That's all?"

"How about you?"

"Nine hundred days."

"Wow."

"A little longer, actually."

"Wow, that's a long time—but don't you get tired of hanging out with the same person?"

"Not with her."

"For me the longest was two months. Even one month is a challenge. I'll be done with this guy before long."

"That's not dating, you're just fooling around."

"Then what about you—you go out for nine hundred days then call it quits just like that?"

"You wouldn't understand—you're too young."

"Only a year younger than you."

"Congratulations—a year younger, that's wonderful."

Crystal crushes out the cigarette. Minho rests an arm on the back of her chair. She brings her feet up to the seat of her chair, buries her head between her upraised knees, and whimpers like a puppy. Minho leans closer. The evening breeze from off the nearby hill is ice cold. Goose bumps break out on her arms. Minho smooths her hair. She looks at him. They regard each other with no display of emotion. A long pause, the two of them drawing out the time. Minho's arm comes to rest on the armrest of her chair. His gaze bores into her cheek. He says, "I'm out of here." And ever so faintly her face clouds over. He gets up. She drops her feet to the floor, extends her arms straight ahead, stretching. He takes one of her arms and lifts it then passes under it. She grabs the armrests and holds tight, her eyes following him. Wanting him to look back and see her watching him. Just then he turns and looks back at her. She gets up. Scurrying after him she takes his arm. "Bye. Are you okay if I don't go down with you?"

"Sure. You know, that T-shirt, it's really…"

"Really what?" She looks down at her T-shirt and meets Dumbo's eyes. "What about it?"

"It's kind of silly…in a cute way, I mean."

"Yeah, it is cute. I totally love it."

He laughs. "See ya."

"Bye."

The door closes and Crystal, arms folded, paces back and forth for a time. A gentle smile spreads across her face. She runs to her room and throws herself on her bed. The bed rumbles and the next moment it's still.

WOULD YOU BE MY FUCKING BOYFRIEND?

His monitor's wide screen is a patchwork of black-and-white images. Lying sideways on Crystal's bed, shoulder propped against a pillow, Minho stares at it. Sitting cross-legged beside him and chewing on her pencil eraser, Crystal looks between the screen and the workbook lying open on the floor.

"*Oppa*, can you help me with this?" She points at the workbook.

He regards it seriously, then checks the title. "I'm in the liberal arts track. I don't do this stuff."

"And I'm in the science track, so I don't watch movies like that."

"Why not? You've got spiral stairs, you've got vertigo. Isn't that scientific?"

"No way! That guy's a pervert, a psycho, he's out of his mind, a dirty old man…." She checks his reaction. "Could you possibly understand what makes that guy tick?"

"Yeah. You don't?"

"You really do… Gee."

"Gee." Minho mimics her and laughs.

Crystal scowls. "I'm going there during school break."

"Where?"

She points at the monitor, "There. Saen—P'ran—shisk'o."

"Just to check it out?"

"No, for English camp. But yeah, it's really an excuse to have fun."

Minho draws her close, grinning. Leaning her head against his shoulder she continues chewing on the eraser. He snatches the pencil and tosses it to the floor.

"Hey, you broke off the tip. Now what am I going to do?"

"I'm sleepy."

"Then take a nap." Crystal places a warm hand on his shoulder. Then she cranes her head back and looks up at the ceiling. Before they know it the sun's going down and Crystal's unlit room is steeped in darkness. Except for the monitor everything melts formlessly into the gloom. She buries her face in his shoulder and he takes her hand.

"I'm sleepy."

"I am too, Minho."

Holding her around the waist, he lies back on the bed.

She giggles. "Stop, you're tickling me."

"Tickling?"

"That's what I said."

They both laugh. The laughter trails off and their whispering breaths fill the room. They lie still for a while. Then her cellphone on the desk vibrates. She tries to get up but he holds her close and won't let go. The phone blinks a few more times and then goes dark.

Again the phone vibrates and blinks in the dark. They lie silent and motionless. She can feel his heart beating. She feels it beating faster and faster, feels his hands getting hotter. She grins—it's all perfectly natural, physiology at work. But before long this discovery has become tedious and stale. Her phone vibrates and blinks. She makes another attempt to wriggle free. This time he lets her go, free and easy. She takes the phone and reads the message aloud in a staccato tone: "*What's up? I'm bored. Let's hang out.*"

"Who's that?"

"My boyfriend," she says with a smirk. "Jealous?"

"As if." He yawns, and the next thing she knows, his eyes are shut. Looking down at his long eyelashes and the pretty shadows they cast beneath his eyes, she grins. "You'd look awesome with mascara."

"What?"

"Mascara. Want to give it a try?"

Minho grabs at her arm but she's able to get the phone to her ear. "Who's that?" Minho asks again.

Crystal looks into his eyes and says, "My boyfriend."

"What?"

"Hush." Minho takes Crystal's free hand and tickles the palm. She tries to yank it away, but he doesn't let go.

A voice leaks from the phone. "Hey—where're you at? What're you up to?"

She bursts out laughing and gives Minho a playful slap on the back. Minho moans faintly.

"What's so funny?" comes the voice from the phone.

"Nothing."

"Where're you at? What're you doing?"

"I'm home."

"Come on out."

"No."

"Why not?"

"Listen," she says, looking at Minho. "You and me…why don't we break up?"

"What?"

Minho bursts into laughter. She hits him on the back,

this time harder. He covers his mouth trying to stifle the laughter, but it doesn't work. "Hush!" Her free hand grabs his shoulder and shakes it. "Hush!"

Minho puts his mouth to her ear. "All right," he whispers. "I'll be quiet."

"Shh!"

"What? Say what? Run that by me again."

"Pyŏl—let's cut the cord."

"Crystal, is this some kind of game?"

"No, I'm dead serious." She tries to steady her breathing, but one look at Minho's face and she bursts out giggling. Minho joins in. She's barely able to reel herself back in before continuing.

"We need to break up...yeah...I'm awfully sorry, but let's call it quits. It's not working. Not anymore. I mean we're done. All right? Finished. The end. Closure."

"Hey, hey, hey. Don't hang up. Don't. You do and you're dead. Dead. You, dead."

"Cool it. I'm right here."

Pyŏl is silent. Then Crystal hears him curse loudly in the background, and then the cursing becomes threats. And then he's speaking into the phone again. "What's got into you, Crystal? This is so sudden."

"You really want to know why we need to split up? It's because I'm into someone new."

Another burst of laughter from Minho.

Crystal covers his mouth. "Quiet!"

"What was that? I can't hear you."

"Why do I have to keep repeating myself? I said I have someone else. Don't you get it? Want me to say it in English?"

Another voice comes on the line. "Hey, Crystal, can you tell me what's wrong? Just chill—why don't the two of you meet and talk it over."

"Who is this?"

"I'm a friend of Pyŏl's. He's a good guy, you know."

"I know he's a good guy. Could you put him back on?"

"Sure. Hey, Pyŏl."

"Yeah, like he said, meet me and we can talk."

"What for? Is there anything left to talk about?"

"Who's your new lover boy?"

Minho gets up from the bed. "Bathroom."

Crystal nods. Perched at the edge of the bed, face solemn, she looks at the monitor. The actress—tragic expression and tragic posture—scurries through the garden with a man in pursuit.

"I don't love you," says Crystal.

"I asked who the asshole is."

"It's a girl. Happy now?"

"What girl?"

"Mina."

"You're out of your mind."

"Yes, I am. Crazy in love." She giggles. The woman on the screen jumps from a tower. "Oh my god."

"What?"

"Nothing."

"Crazy bitch."

"No cursing."

"You are a crazy bitch."

"Well, I guess this conversation is over. Bye. Take care. And have a happy life."

"Crazy—"

She snaps the phone shut and tosses it on the bed, then sits primly waiting for Minho.

"Done?"

She nods.

Minho sits down next to her. "Movie's over too."

"That's right."

"How come you're always breaking up with someone when I'm around?"

"Maybe you jinx my relationships."

"What do you mean? I didn't do anything."

"I'm serious. Think about it."

Crystal looks at Minho and smiles. Minho looks at Crystal and smiles. Seeing him smile puts her in a good mood. He has a refreshing smile.

"…Yeah, I like it."

"What?"

"I like it. When you smile, *Oppa*. Smile. Like that. Smile. Yeah, smile. I like it when you smile, *Oppa*."

Again she looks at Minho and smiles. They smile awkwardly at each other, the dark, underhanded grins of accomplices.

"I need to get going on my homework. You ready to go home? I kind of liked the ending of that movie…"

"You're really weird."

"That's why you like me, right?" She pokes him in the arm. "Right? Right? What do you think? I'm right, aren't I? Come on, tell me."

The phone rings. She quickly taps Off and while she's adding Pyŏl's number to her blocked list two texts come in. She reads and deletes them. Another text pops up. This one she deletes without reading. Minho vacantly watches her looking at her phone with a grave expression. She looks up at him. "Want to go for a smoke?"

Minho nods. They cross the living room and go out on the balcony. She takes his left hand in hers and puts it to her cheek. "I love you." He removes his hand and lights up.

"*Oppa*, how come you act like you don't smoke?"

"Well, I don't."

"Then what do you call this?"

"Well, just once in a while."

"So once in a while means you don't smoke?"

"Mmm."

She gives him a sweet smile. "Want to see something?"

"What's that?"

Cigarette in her mouth, she unlocks her phone. "Check this out. See?"

"Wow, he just doesn't give up. You don't mind me seeing these?"

"I don't care if he keeps texting." She scowls.

"What's *that*?"

"A dying kitten."

"What?"

"A dying kitten, that's what." She blows out a cloud of smoke. "Damn, I need to quit smoking."

"Do it then."

"I don't want to. I also filmed it."

"Let me see."

Crystal hits the video replay button and turns up the volume. Against a dark background the little kitten is lying stretched out and moaning. Minho scans the living room. "It was here."

"Mm-hmm."

Crystal's dry voice can be heard: "Hey kitty, don't die, kitty."

"That's you?" Crystal nods. "Your kitten?"

"Nope. Well, it almost was. But it died."

"Did you buy it?"

"No, I found it next to the garbage cans." On the screen Crystal takes the cat by the tail and yanks it. Minho looks on, eyes gleaming with curiosity. With difficulty the kitten lifts its head, bares its teeth, and growls. They hear Crystal's dry laughter. Then her apology. Then her sobbing. Then her laughing. Another apology. A scene from the theater of the absurd transplanted into the twenty-first century.

"Wait a minute—are you sure it was dying?"

"Positive."

"But why'd you film it? And how'd it die? Did something happen?"

"I killed it, that's how."

Minho stares at her.

"It's true. I killed it. What do you have to say to that? Tell me. Now that you've seen it, maybe you don't like me anymore."

"Am I supposed to stop liking you now that I've seen that?"

She nods. "That's what happened with Mina. She said she doesn't like me anymore."

"It's a big world. Why don't you find yourself some new friends."

"No need. Now that I have you, *Oppa*."

Smiling, Minho puts his arms around her and draws her close.

"You watched me break up with him. I did that for you, *Oppa*, because I love you, *Oppa*."

Minho replays the video. "But why did you do that? How could you kill a kitten? A cat would be hard to kill, wouldn't it?"

"I threw it against the wall. A bunch of times." She stubs out her cigarette and snatches her phone from him. "That's enough. It's not exactly wholesome entertainment for a kid."

Suddenly Crystal flies into a rage. She walks out onto the balcony and kicks the railing: one, two, three, four, five times.

Minho watches her, unnerved.

"It's invincible! Okay. Done with your smoke? Then let's get you on your way."

Minho has no idea what's just happened. But he doesn't wonder and so he doesn't question her about it.

No attempt to understand. Keeping silent. That's the lifestyle he's chosen. It keeps things simple and peaceful. He doesn't write down or talk about anything. His thoughts drift from left to right and fly off in the company of the wind and dust. Day after day passes in the same fashion. Time flies and there are no worries. You could simply say that he's thought-less and opinion-less. If you were to say that to him he would of course protest, saying: *No, I'm more complicated than that, I'm smart, I think all day, I'm maybe a bit nastier than you think, a bit more esoteric, a bit more tainted, a bit more sensitive.* But that's his misunderstanding. He's inclined to over-rate himself, just like any schoolboy. He doesn't talk simply because he has nothing to say. Being taciturn is indicative of a one-dimensional brain. Being polite is indicative of an apathetic heart. When he has nothing to say, instead of trying to think of something, he just keeps his mouth shut. He started out keeping quiet because he had nothing to say, but because he never said anything he grew more and more quiet. He's ever more thought-less and opinion-less, and all the more charming for it. His skin, pale throughout the summer, and his fine bone structure and lean physique, just right for a T-shirt and jeans, coalesce into charm and mystique in the eyes of others, particularly schoolgirls. On the other hand, with those he's attracted to he's loquacious and mischievous, even a bit of a risk-taker, and is inclined to be direct. But this side of him is veiled in politeness and doesn't come across as rash and, because of his taciturn manner, is considered a conscious choice on his part. His lifestyle defies any comprehensive value judgment. Indeed, it makes him an archetype of a contemporary kid, and this is the very reason Crystal and Minho are attracted to each other.

Basically, Crystal and Minho are cut from the same cloth. They don't understand why people behave the way they do, and they don't try to find out. She has no clue what he thinks, but is fine with that since she's not interested in the first place. She thinks it's good if he smiles and bad if he frowns. But he always smiles, so there's no problem there. They say nothing of substance and ask nothing of each other; Crystal cares about no one but Crystal, and Minho cares about no one but Minho. They expect nothing. The only thing that surprises them is the numbness and frigidity they read in each other's eyes. Nothing else. Even though they don't really talk, they somehow believe they know each other. From childhood on, they've observed that kids behave exactly how they'd expect them to act, and that knowledge feels like the tedious pleasure that comes at the end of a chess game. They are creatures of habit. Habitually silent. Like animals who, lacking language, are at peace in silence while cradling each other's head. Watching them you might think that theirs is the most platonic of relationships, noble and innocent. Because they look so beautiful listening attentively to each other's breathing, an arm draped over the other's bare neck. A pair of unripe bodies and souls left defenseless in the pale shroud of dusk, they're more radiant and beautiful than the brilliant sunlight of May. Their youth itself is lovely, their immaturity enticing. But at the same time, their brains are still contaminated by language and so their relationship is limited to a game of tempting and being tempted. They are animals who possess language and can't live without it. They only pretend to ignore and exclude it. They're far removed from the type of primal relationship that preceded language—a genuine, idealized relationship. For them it's still all about the social graces and sterilizing their environment to avoid contamination, like spreading a white napkin over your lap in a restaurant. Minho doesn't ask Crystal questions, and Crystal doesn't ask Minho questions about not questioning her. And thus nothing happens. The hours draw out silently. Not the sort of life to inspire a soul. Can you save a soul only by leaning a body against a body and repeatedly embracing? Can the mind expand in such hours? More likely they will stubbornly stay the same, in the same pose with the same expression. They'll spend as long as they can leaning against each other in silence, then simply wave goodbye once it's time for cram school.

These empty hours are of no comfort to Crystal at a moment like this. Instead of saying she's angry she kicks the balcony railing instead, as an indirect expression of her anger. And Minho would consider it an invasion of privacy if he asked her why she kicked the railing, choosing to assume it was to test its strength. It's a tradition in his family not to criticize people's behavior, whatever they might do, but to accept it graciously as a mark of individuality. It's a point of pride in Minho's family. These values are held not just by his parents but by the entire extended family and even his parents' friends. Accepting another person's behavior no matter what. Accepting. Accepting. They've always thought of it as *accepting*. His parents smile, proud and satisfied at having created an atmosphere of respect for everyone, but all it has really amounted to is their children being insensitive to others.

Crystal is still fuming. Minho finds her cute and charming when she's like this.

"Bye—you don't need to walk me out."

"I wasn't planning on it."

He grins. She thinks his leather messenger bag looks good on him. He gives an exaggerated wave, and the door closes. Her smile quickly vanishes and she gazes desperately at the door. *Come back, come back, open the door and give me a nice big smile.* But the door doesn't open. Her cellphone vibrates with a new text. She takes it from her pocket and drops it on the floor as if flicking away a speck of dust. The sturdy phone withstands the impact. She picks it up and throws it to the floor. It breaks in two. She repeats the process, then finds her father's hiking boots, puts them on, and proceeds to stomp on what's left. Hand against the wall, trying to steady her breathing, she keeps stomping on the shattered phone. *I can't help it.*

A moment later she looks down at the fragments. Heaving a sigh, she makes a circuit of the living room, retrieving the sofa cushions from the floor and tidying the magazines on the coffee table, then she stretches before heading to the kitchen. For a while there's only the sound of her busy footsteps. Then she reappears holding a large plastic bag. Kneeling on the floor, she gathers what's left of the phone and puts it into the bag. Suddenly she cries out and sticks her thumb in her mouth. She scurries into her parents' room. There's the sound of drawers opening and shutting. She returns to the living room with a Band-Aid. Carefully she wraps it around her thumb. She ties the bag securely and tosses it in the trash. Then she sits down on the sofa and turns on the TV. The image of a folksy comedian fills the screen. From time to time she breaks out giggling and rubs her bandaged thumb. She suddenly gets up, puts the ashtray full of cigarette butts on the balcony, then sits back on the sofa and makes a call on the landline.

"Hi Mom, it's me. Mmm. Know what? I lost my phone… I was out by the river with a friend and thought it'd be cool to take a boat ride. No, with Mina. Yes, I finished my homework. Yes, I ate. Stuffed. Totally. It fell into the ocean—I mean the river. What? Yes, of course I'm telling you the truth. How am I supposed to find it? You know it wouldn't work anymore, don't you? What can I do? I'm sorry, Mom. What—we still owe on it? How can that be? Oh, no. What am I going to do? Mom, I'm *totally* sorry. Mm-hmm. Could I possibly use your old one? I know. Okay, tomorrow then?… I'm leaving for cram school twenty…eight minutes from now. Mm-hmm. Mom, I'm so, so sorry. Mom? One more thing. I'd really love some sweet-and-sour pork. Mm-hmm. I know. Love you too."

Putting the phone on the floor, she lies down on the sofa. Raising her right hand high, she works her thumb as if texting. Just then the doorbell rings.

"Who is it?"

"Hey, it's me. Can you come out?" Pyŏl's low-pitched, fretful voice over the intercom sounds louder than it actually is in the tranquility of the living room.

"What are you doing here? Go home. I'm about to go to cram…"

"Get out here, now!" he growls, his voice still low-pitched but menacing now.

Chewing on her thumbnail, she stares at the intercom's screen. Against the gloom of the background Pyŏl looks dark green. He's facing away from the screen. His stubborn jawline catches her eye. She wonders what he's looking at.

"Wait there."

Outside on the steps to the building she finds him smoking a cigarette. Two middle-aged women with grocery baskets pass by with disapproving but slightly fearful expressions, then cut through the complex.

"If they catch you smoking in your school uniform, they'll kick you out."

"Why should I be worried? I don't live around here."

"They'll report you to the police."

"Let them."

"What were you looking at when you rang the doorbell?" Crystal looks around. "The playground? That's the only possibility. Is that where you were looking instead of at me?"

Pyŏl gets to his feet and crushes out his cigarette, and the next thing Crystal knows he's snatched her by the wrist and is dragging her. She struggles to free herself but her arm feels like a log. With her eyes wide and her mouth gaping she's pulled toward the entrance of the complex.

"You're hurting me!" she manages to scream. He stops and lets go of her. Holding her wrist close, she plops down, squatting just above the ground.

"You okay? Did I hurt your arm?"

She glares at him. "Fuck you!"

Stunned by the obscenity, he's momentarily speechless. And then he says, "Sorry, Crystal. I'm sorry. Sorry."

"Where are you trying to take me? Tell me."

"I just want to go somewhere and talk."

"There's nothing to talk about."

"There is for me."

"Well what do you know. I guess there is—for you." She raises the wrist Pyŏl was holding and shakes it to get the circulation going again, while considering her options.

"What happened to your thumb?"

"What about it?"

He takes her hand and examines it, rubbing the bandaged thumb.

"Don't do that."

"Sorry. Does it hurt? How did it happen?"

"A knife." The look she gives him is blank.

"You cut yourself?"

"An accident. A stupid mistake." Again she shakes her wrist.

"What are you doing?"

"Thinking."

"About what?"

Okay... she mumbles, *I guess I can skip first period.* Then she looks at him. "This is when I should be going to cram school, right? But I've decided to skip first period—because of *you.* How about that? Going to thank me or what?" Pyŏl is about to say something but she makes a hushing gesture. "Never mind. It's okay. Let's get a cab. I'm beat. Oh, here comes one now. Good timing."

He flags down the cab and hustles to open the door for her. She takes off her backpack and holds it to her chest as she climbs in.

"H Department Store, please."

Neither of them speak. She's busy massaging her wrist. He grips his wallet with both hands, looking down at it. She sags against the window and gnaws at her thumb. The taxi keeps hitting red lights. Pyŏl sighs. Crystal sighs. The driver glances at them in the rearview mirror and sighs too. From the radio comes Sim Soo-bong singing "Quizas, Quizas, Quizas." The very moment it ends, the DJ comes on with a breaking story: "The North has just conducted another nuclear test in Hamgyŏng Province. The precise location, type, and scale of the test have yet to be confirmed, and…" The DJ's voice trails off. Her bright, breezy tone seems out of place. Another song comes on, and this time is interrupted mid-play. A newscaster comes on and repeats the same breaking story in a stiff tone.

The next light turns red and the cab slows to a stop. "Traffic!" The driver beats the steering wheel lightly. The newscaster goes on to report that the U.S. has decided to step up its economic sanctions against the North, South Korea has decided to suspend humanitarian food aid, and the U.N. has unanimously adopted a strongly worded resolution condemning the North's action. During the commercials that follow, the three occupants remain silent. Crystal tells the driver to stop. Pyŏl takes some money from his wallet. Crystal gets out and walks off while Pyŏl is getting change, nodding to the driver, and closing the door. He runs after her. She's already inside a small cake shop in an alley.

"No smoking in here," she reminds him when they're both seated.

The waitress brings Crystal a banana smoothie and cheesecake and Pyŏl gets a sumptuous cappuccino.

Spooning the foam into his mouth, Pyŏl says, "This is my dinner."

"I've got to be in class in fifty minutes. So talk."

Pyŏl continues spooning foam.

"You like the cappuccino? I bet. They use fair-trade organic beans from Jamaica, you know. But give it a rest and tell me what you want to say."

"It's all my fault. I won't do it again." His voice is artificially buoyant, as if he knows how awkward the words sound.

"Who told you to apologize? I sure didn't."

"Chŏngu—"

"Oh, so this was Chŏngu's idea? Okay. Wrong move. I never would have figured him to suggest something like that. From now on I don't think you should hang out with him."

"What the hell! Why are you doing this to me? It's all just a game, isn't it? And all that business about a new lover… that's a big fat lie, too, right?"

"Did Chŏngu feed you these questions too? Come on, spill it."

"Spill what?"

"Let me see the script he wrote for you."

"No such thing!"

"C'mon…you've got to have it somewhere.… Let's just stop. This is a pain."

"A pain, huh? Do I sound like I'm bullshitting you?"

"There you go again with your dirty mouth."

"All right. Sorry. No swearing. I won't do it again."

"Why not? You can swear all you want, for all I care."

She cocks her head and smiles. He heaves a sigh, then glares at her. She feels a tinge of fear but forces herself to sit ramrod straight as she sips her smoothie.

"Let's be honest."

"I am."

"Who is it?"

"Who is what?"

"Who's the guy you say you're in love with?"

"You don't need to know."

"Why not?"

"Why should I tell you?"

"Did he say he loves you too?"

"Nope. It's just me and my big crush on him."

"Crazy bitch. Just fucking listen to you."

Unfazed, she leans in close to him. "You want to die? I *told* you not to swear."

"Okay. Sorry." He looks at her wide-eyed.

Crystal cuts her cheesecake into small pieces with her fork. "Think about it. You and I have known each other for less than a month. You really think that's long enough for things to get serious?"

"Hey…"

"He's different than you. He doesn't like me, see? But you do. You messaged me: 'I loving you more and more.' It was ungrammatical, like a bad translation, don't you remember? But I'm sorry to say, I don't like you. Let me say it again: I don't like you. I like him, but he doesn't like me. Well, maybe I *don't* like him. What does it even mean to like someone? It's stupid. At least I've made up my mind to like him. But I could never make up my mind to like you. I've made up my mind to like him, even if he hasn't made up his mind about me yet. But he smiles when he looks at me. He's a good guy, he walks the line. He doesn't let himself like anyone who doesn't fit the same profile—and I sure don't. But he looks at me and smiles anyway. He never frowns. Even when I do something he doesn't like. But I know why he's the way he is. I do. Excuse me…could I have a latte, please? No syrup, and could you make it soy? Not too much, please. I find him amazing. That's where it stands now, and we've only just begun, things are going to pick up."

Pyŏl drops his spoon. He bends over to pick it up from the floor.

"Hey, don't do that. It's dirty. Could we have another spoon, please? I'm dizzy. I'm talking too much and being way too nice, which I'm not really crazy about. So, your turn.

Go ahead. Oh…I'm getting dizzy again."

"Frankly…" He looks hesitantly at Crystal.

"Say it, I'm all ears… So dizzy."

"Frankly…I don't understand a thing you just said. So, what are…so you think I'm…"

"That is why I can't love you. When you don't understand something, you should just smile. Why do you need to ask all these questions? How can I remember everything I said—I'm already done saying it. You should have listened more carefully, you know?"

"It's no fun listening to you, since you're always talking shit."

"Hey, lower your voice. And keep it low."

Pyŏl lowers his voice to a whisper. "It's no fun listening to you always talk shit."

She bursts into laughter.

"What's so funny?'

"I didn't mean for you to whisper."

The server sets a slender mug of latte in front of her. Crystal gives her a sweet smile of thanks then quickly erases it from her face. Expressionless, with her chin cupped in her palm, she looks at Pyŏl. This entire sequence is going off without a hitch—she's skilled enough that she should be drawing sighs from onlookers.

Her irises are unusually dark and large. In those serene and impassive eyes it would be hard to find any trace of feeling or meaning. Pyŏl doesn't like it when she looks at him with her eyes like this. It puts him in a bad mood. No, it's more than just a bad mood, he tells himself. He focuses in an effort to find the words to describe this delicate, elusive feeling, but nothing comes. But he's sure that if it was a boy who was stupid enough to look at him like she is, he'd spit in the

kid's face and then hit him as hard as he could. Until this moment he's never had to agonize over what to do in a situation
like this. The other girls he's gone out with weren't like this.
That's why he likes Crystal. But the Crystal sitting before him
now seems more risky than attractive—too much of a risk,
really. But she is very pretty, he has to admit as she savors her
latte. He tries to think of what to say, but it's not easy.

"You don't look too good." The next moment he wishes
he hadn't said it.

"Really? I'm fine."

"Well, to me you seem a little…off."

"It's because I'm lovesick." She cocks her head again,
looking up in the air dreamily. Pyŏl is just about to be sucked
into the blinding, lustrous mood she's created, but jumps free
at the last instant. He's seriously conflicted: Should he slap
her? His eyes meet hers and his face burns. She's grinning
from ear to ear. He imagines himself slowly raising his fist
and sending it flying into her cheek. She's knocked to the
other side of the booth. Buries her head in her arms and
moans. Her cheek turning whiter around the darkening impression of his fist. Tears dangling from her eyes then raining
to the table.

Now his hands are on the table, palms down, and he
looks at them, startled. He closes them into fists and glares at
her. He's about to say something, then stops. He taps the table
lightly with his knuckles.

"What, you going to hit me?"

"Why would I do that?"

With an awkward smile he holds out his hands. She
jerks backward, frightened. Embarrassed again, he erases
the smile. Frozen stiff, they consider each other fearfully. He
looks into her eyes—desperately. She avoids his gaze and

keeps her eyes on his mug of cappuccino—desperately.

"You'd never hit me. You won't even touch me."

Hearing her meek, quivering voice, he chuckles.

"Go ahead and laugh. If that's all you can do."

"Crazy bitch."

Pretending not to have heard, she flashes a smile and extends her arms, stretching. "Ahhhh, once more…ahhhh. A cup of coffee and I feel like I'm ready for anything. It's a great feeling. Let's hear it for caffeine. Okay, all better now. So, I'm off. How about you? You all right? You're good?"

Crystal rises and offers him a killer smile. Her eyes check their surroundings then circle back. She leans in close and whispers in his ear, "Don't you ever call me again. I'll kill you if you do. I mean it. I will kill you, you fucking bastard."

She looks up and around them again. A few people had been watching her but they quickly look away to avoid meeting her eyes. *Everything's working out just fine*, she thinks as she eases outside and heads toward cram school.

"I'm sorry, kids, but it looks like you're going to lose your English comp instructor. He says he wants to go back home."

"How come?"

"Did he give a reason?"

"Why?"

"I don't know for sure. But he says he's going home. He's afraid of North Korea. Says he's not going to stay any longer."

"Really? But why now?"

"Are you sure?"

"That's bull."

"He's a chicken."

"I thought he was cute—what a letdown."

"I don't really know if it's about the North. I don't actually know why. Wasn't his contract up next month anyway?"

"That's news to me."

"Who said that?"

"So, who's going to teach us?"

"Why don't you go ask the director."

"Let him go if he wants," Crystal shouts. "Let him. Life's a scary business. Maybe he should give it up. Lock himself inside and hide under his bed. Let him go back to the U.S. He'll be gunned down there and then so long, Mike."

Everyone falls silent.

"I mean, what's happening? I hate what's going on in the world. It's absurd. What a joke!"

Noticing that her classmates are waiting to hear what she'll say next, Crystal breaks off and looks instead at the instructor. "Aren't we supposed to be having class?"

The teacher's face turns white as a sheet. She's about to say something, then shakes her head and moves on to the lesson.

The classroom is unusually subdued. Crystal is the only one who's really into the class—though her classmates would probably say she's too intense. Today in particular there's a lot she's wondering about, so much that she's having trouble understanding. She's asking all the questions, then nodding compulsively while the instructor answers. Backpack held tight to her chest, left leg jiggling, she frantically takes notes, never pausing. The instructor feels a wisp of fear. Crystal zips through the problems. Her dogged bombardment of questions finally brings her to an understanding about the problems. Disconcerted by Crystal and unable to get a grip on the problems, the other students bury their heads in their workbooks and scribble numbers. The instructor's fear rises. The white, windowless classroom is a sea of fluorescent light. Everyone except Crystal feels an unpleasant warmth in the air. The instructor's face reddens and beads of perspiration appear. She fans her face with a folded piece of paper. Suddenly Crystal points to a > sign written on the board. "That's wrong."

"I can't believe how disrespectful you are!" the instructor shouts. She's surprised by her own voice, which strikes her as hysterical. Leaning against her desk for support, she takes a deep breath.

Again Crystal points out her error. "It should be pointing the other way, shouldn't it? It's the wrong symbol."

The teacher glares at her. "No, it's not."

"Yes, it is."

"No, it's not."

"It doesn't make sense…. Take your time and think about it." Crystal heaves a dramatic sigh. "How can that side be greater? Look at the graph…"

"It *is* greater."

"You're trying to trick us."

"Crystal, leave the room."

"Why me? You're the one who should leave."

The instructor's face contorts.

"I mean, why should I have to leave?"

"Hey, that's enough," says another girl, giving Crystal's shoulder a shove and smiling awkwardly at the instructor. "Tell her you're sorry." And to the instructor, "Sorry about that. I think she's just upset because Mike's leaving."

Crystal slaps the girl. With a scream the girl grabs Crystal's arm and twists it.

"Ow!" says Crystal with a slight frown. "Let go—I'm asking you nicely."

"Let her go. Don't waste your time fighting with a girl like her. Crystal, I want you to leave, now. I'm not telling you again. Get out and stay out till class is over. Wait for me downstairs." The instructor grimaces, then looks up at the ceiling, fanning herself. "Unbelievable... My god...hey... what is your problem? Get out, now!"

"No." Crystal bursts into tears. "No! I won't! I'm not leaving!" And she pounds her desk, sobbing.

The instructor comes over to Crystal, reaches out, takes her by the shoulder, and in the flattest voice she can summon says: "Get out, right now." Her tone is cold but somehow plaintive. Her life and her job have left her with an overwhelming sense of remorse. She feels tears coming but desperately holds them off. Steadying her breathing, she tells herself to be strong. *Don't lower yourself to their level.* She chants this mantra in an attempt to remind herself of her superiority over her adversaries.

The reason you're crying is you haven't learned to hold in your tears, you're not used to it. But you'll learn if you want to survive. In order to survive, you'll learn. And then you won't cry anymore. You'll end up dry and sterile just like me. Life is disgusting, it really is. You don't really know it yet but one of these days you'll find yourself up to your knees in muck, I guarantee it. Yes I do. And when that happens you'll see that you're just as ugly and disgusting as I am, or even worse. That's why I'm not angry with you now. But I won't offer to help you. I'll just watch as you wade into the rising muck.

Poised over Crystal's bowed head, the instructor unleashes her silent curse. Crystal's sad weeping grows louder and louder, expressing opposition to everyone in the class; it is extremely annoying. The instructor does her best to remain undeterred. Steadying her trembling legs, she puts on a stoic face and looks around the classroom. The lovely, dough-white faces of the kids are filled with fear and worry. They mostly look stupefied. Seeing their faces, the instructor feels another surge of rage, but she vows to use that anger to press on; she *has* to move on. She has absolutely no intention of canceling the remainder of class. Her hair is long, lustrous, and untreated by dyes or chemicals. Sweeping it back with her hand, she returns to her position at her desk in front of the board.

"Let's get on with class. Please ignore her."

Crystal emits a long, feeble sob. With clenched teeth the instructor erases the chalkboard. Hesitantly the kids look up at the board. As the instructor flips through the workbook a sheet of paper falls out. A boy springs out of his seat and picks it up for her. "Thank you," she says with a controlled smile. In a strained voice she launches into an explanation of logarithmic functions. She mentions the three types that appear the least frequently on the university entrance exam, adding a mechanized dash of humor by giggling. She follows by explaining the seven types that appear most frequently. This time the humor comes in the form of a joke, and this time the students laugh. *Success.* Crystal gets up and thrashes around as she gathers her things in her backpack. Marching toward the door, she turns and points to the instructor. "You're wrong."

Crystal slams the door as hard as she can and flinches, startled by the bang, then puts her head down and scuttles down the hallway, passing kids who hover about: kids saying "hi" to each other; kids sipping on cans of juice from the vending machine; kids resting their feet on chairs while they listen to their MP3 players and tackle workbook assignments; kids who call her name; and kids pushing and being pushed through the cram school's front door. Another person hollers her name. Not responding, she rushes out to the street.

It's already dark. She heads for the city center and blends into the crowds on the busy streets. Glaring at the signs layering the buildings, she feels another surge of rage she can't explain. Too many people here. Passing through the crowd, she feels her anger building. She marches along quickly, just like everyone else. Where she is, everyone's in a hurry, pushing and shoving and bumping shoulders. Not to be rude but just to keep up with the frenetic pace of the city. The metropolis encourages its residents to be less polite, more selfish; it has no room for manners. Not wanting to be left out, the people have to move more aggressively, pushing others out of their way.

Narrow alleys radiate left and right from the streets. She remembers those alleys and turns down them one by one. They contain a dizzying array of shops. Optic nerves on high alert, she registers each and every piece of merchandise. Her gaze lingers briefly on an appetizing cheese muffin. And then on a graceful, frilly green dress. Then a pair of open-toed shoes with crystal beads. A white mannequin in a navy suit holding a For Sale sign at its chest. In this gigantic catalog of a commercial district, Crystal plays the role of a young student with a dark, oversize backpack who is window-shopping. She fits in perfectly with the merchandise from the catalog. Like the other shoppers, she picks out those items worth trying on. But there are too many people. And dust. More people. Lights. More dust. A woman of breathtaking, almost artificial beauty brushes past her, trailing a heavy floral scent. Her short, unadorned orange dress highlights her long and slender limbs. All eyes come together on her before rebounding the next moment. A man turns and gives her a wishful look. Crystal glances back at the woman as well but meets the eyes of the man. He turns away. The woman fades into the distance. This is exactly what people mean when they speak of Beauty. Deflated, Crystal considers her own clothes—T-shirt, jeans, sneakers, and backpack—nothing out of the ordinary. She recalls Minho smiling at the sight of Dumbo on her T-shirt and finds herself yearning for him. She reaches for her phone before remembering it's in pieces in the trash. *I need a new one.* She walks into a phone store and checks out the sleek new models. Back outside, heavyhearted, she looks for a phone booth but on impulse goes into an Adidas outlet instead. She's in the middle of downtown, and the shop is in a three-story landmark building. The interior is calm, and the merchandise is spaced out nicely in a way that's easy on the eye. Intently she examines each of the items. She starts with the garments she has no interest in, checking the price tags with a determined look as if she's about to try them on or buy them on the spot. A saleswoman approaches and asks if she needs help. Smiling, she shakes her head no. Next it's backpacks. She touches each of the ones that she's already decided are ugly, then tries them on and looks in the mirror to compare. She's relieved to see she looks normal, but the sight of her face makes her want to throw up or break the mirror. *It's all right.* She manages to brace herself. In her own backpack she finds her purse and looks inside—seven thousand *wŏn* and a credit card. Putting her purse away, she resumes her inspection of the backpacks, this time even more seriously. The saleswoman approaches again, this time with a variety of questions. Crystal keeps nodding, acting dumb and gnawing on her fingernails. The woman gives up and backs off. And then, square in the middle of the shop, Crystal discovers a huge dark gray messenger bag. It's made by a trendy young American female designer, and the price is outrageous. She likes the bag, but try as she might she can't think of an excuse to buy it. She looks around and catches the saleswoman's eye. The woman comes over, straps the bag over Crystal's shoulder, and guides her to the mirror. Crystal turns in a slow circle, seeing how it looks on her. With the same dumb expression as before, she glares into the mirror, and the woman asks if she'd like to buy it. Crystal nods, and the woman brings her to the cashier.

Black shopping bag over her shoulder, she makes her leisurely way back through the alleys. Pausing in front of a bakery, she zeroes in on a beautiful raspberry tart. She resumes her walk. She changes direction. Changes direction again. Stops countless times to look at things in shop windows. She doesn't know what to do, which is a kind of torture. Gazing into the bright windows, she waits for a directive to appear. No such luck. She resumes walking. Her back is moist with cold sweat. She's dizzy and hungry. Her feet are heavy and her calf muscles burn. But she doesn't stop. She comes to a crosswalk just as the light turns green. Across the street, she goes down into a basement arcade. The smell of soggy *kimpap* is in the air. Holding her breath, she checks out a selection of cheap sunglasses in one of the stalls. She leaves the arcade. Back at street level she finds herself in front of the Adidas shop again. Afraid that other people might think she's weird for circling the same spot, she dashes off. She changes direction several more times and now she's heading west. She looks up as a bus passes by. She weaves through lines of people as they wait at the bus stop. They look worn and tired but are well dressed, giving off gentle fragrances. She drops down into another basement arcade and makes a quick circuit, wondering where to go and what to do. She stops at a snack shop to study the menu, but when an older woman approaches to beckon her inside, she runs off, startled. Leaving the arcade, she keeps walking, in the process crossing who knows how many crosswalks. She looks around and once again she finds herself in front of the Adidas shop. *Okay, I give up.* Eyes half shut and thoughts suspended, she slowly walks away. Suddenly a wide avenue jumps into sight. Beyond it a gigantic, pure white department store looms. It's flanked on both sides by coffee shops of the same chain, identical in size and design. She checks her wristwatch. Taking her MP3 player from her pocket, she puts on her headphones and pushes Play. Cranking the volume all the way up, she resumes her meandering. As soon as the music comes on, the atmosphere's pressure feels different. The next moment, reality is gone. Crystal detaches from her surroundings, teleporting to a fantasy world of nothing but the music. The streets remain rife with noise, but she hears none of it. There's only the strong, swelling music controlling her brain. The streets, the people, the cars, the entire city still moves incessantly, but no longer to its own rhythm but rather to the rhythm Crystal chooses. A single song—the one that's on now—resonates throughout the city. Like the songs before it and the ones that will follow, it brings her catharsis. She's walking through a city controlled by her chosen music. All other aural information has been blocked out, but that's fine with her, because such information is merely white noise that floods the senses and gives nothing of value. What is important is the music. Crystal smiles. No thoughts are intruding. Her soul lifts steadily. It's so beautiful she wants to stop and scream. She closes her eyes. Then opens them. She wonders how many fabulous things have shouldered their way into her consciousness only to disappear in the blink of an eye. She stops at a bench, sets down the shopping bag, and takes out her new messenger bag. She takes off her backpack, unzips it, and dumps the contents into the new bag. She then stuffs her backpack in as well, zips it up, adjusts the shoulder strap, and puts it on. She checks her watch again then crosses more crosswalks and changes direction more times, finally catching sight of the cram school sign in the distance. She stops right in the middle of the alley. Passersby glance her way. But Crystal can't hear a thing. She's all alone. Her spirit is not out in the open like her body, but in the sound. In a soft voice she sings along with the music:

> *All you need is your own imagination*
> *So use it, that's what it's for*
> *Go inside, for your finest inspiration*
> *Your dreams will open the door*

It's an exciting, energizing song. She closes her eyes, turning into where the sound comes from. *Fine,* thinks Crystal, *let's dance in a green field.* She imagines new dance moves; wonders if she would make a good choreographer. She's happy. But anxious. She wonders where the anxiety is coming from. As she considers this day in the life of Crystal, she feels weird. But she's unable to pinpoint what's weird, why it should be weird, and in what exact way it's weird, and that makes her more anxious. But then…bingo: all that caffeine.

She remembers the rich, foaming latte at the cake shop. *All thanks to Pyŏl.* A surge of anger, but she'll manage. Refusing Madonna's invitation to dance, she hits Next:

> *Gimme that old fashion morphine*
> *Gimme that old fashion morphine*
> *Gimme that old fashion morphine*
> *It's good enough for me*

Again the Next button.

I'm waiting for my man
Twenty-six dollars in my hand
Up to Lexington, 125
Feeling sick and dirty, more dead than alive
I'm waiting for my man

Hmm, they're all like this...they're all the same. Waiting for my man? All I need is imagination and old morphine. I'm waiting for my man. Waiting for him to arrive. Twenty-six dollars? Works for me.... It's time to make a new plan. How about a month at a resort in the South Pacific? Hmm, that would screw up my studies. What if I took my workbooks? Nah, a month is way too long. Maybe a week? Summer vacation with my parents? No problem. But what about Minho? Summer vacation with Minho? Oh, that'd be awesome. I wonder what he's up to over summer break.

The next moment it occurs to her that she has to go to ESL camp in San Francisco over summer break. Suddenly she detests San Francisco. With a long face she starts to cross a crosswalk. A motorcycle passes by with a deafening roar. The noise and the vibration and the music join into an indistinguishable clamor. She looks up to see clouds tinted orange and purple from the polluted air. In those clouds she sees the decadent beauty of the adults and the frail, pathological beauty that exists in every city. The thousands of rippling neon lights reflect the decadent beauty of the grown-ups. Everything between heaven and earth shines with their decadence. And Crystal makes her way through that decadence. The streets continue without end. Dust clings to her sweaty skin. She wonders what she should be thinking about, and about what she should do. Fragments of the day's scenes shower down on her, in no particular order. Rage simmers and steeps inside her. To delay it she sings along with a song, this time loudly.

But the artless attempt is no use. She tries as best she can to crumple up today's events. With incredible speed she digs a tunnel deep in the corner of her mind and buries the crumpled remains, essentially un-happening them. And then she tamps the earth down over the mouth of the tunnel, leaving no trace. She removes a tiny fragment from her memory. Files it down and smooths its jagged edge. *A simple operation.* Her thought processes allow such conclusions. Miscalculations are to be expected but she's confident she can fix them. But her rage, having reached a wall, has found a way out, an exit that involved breaking her internal laws. She tries to ignore it. To avoid thinking about anything she fixates on the act of walking. The next moment her hands disappear. *Wow!* Again she focuses, and now she feels her arms, chest, and stomach disappearing. Next it's her head and her calves and thighs. Last to go are the knees and ankles. All that remain are her two feet, which continue to advance.

It's impossible to know how many shops, crosswalks, alleys, and homes she's passed.

But nowhere is there a park with a fountain, or a district where elderly musicians play lively tunes, or benches occupied by people reading books. This is the true face of P City. No metropolis embraces that which doesn't conform. The moment Crystal stops is the moment she'll have to pay for something. Her only option is to keep moving. Moving without rest until she can no longer stand straight, at which point she crawls aboard the first bus she sees.

Lilac bushes line both sides of the path that extends from the bus stop to the entrance of the complex where Mina lives. The lush masses of white and purple blossoms trail like clusters of grapes from the branches, exuding a smothering fragrance more akin to the smell of honey than flowers. The path goes gradually uphill, enough to get Crystal huffing and puffing. The thick scent makes it harder for her to breathe. She imagines being suffocated by the scent—her vision blurring, collapsing to the ground, gasping for air, then convulsions and death. And all the painful stages in between. The path changes directions and the thickets of lilac give way to black locust. Low, well-pruned shrubs are blocked off in tidy squares: pines, cherry trees, and magnolias are situated on the well-tended lawns. Arc-sodium lights illuminate the path in yellow. The apartment complex emerges in the distance. Minho is standing in front by a bench watching her. He flashes the grin she finds so refreshing.

She takes cigarettes from her messenger bag, offers one to him, and lights one for herself. They come together tête-à-tête and the end of her lit cigarette lights his. Sitting on the bench, she rests a hand gently on his shoulder and lowers her head onto it. He pulls her close.

"I have a headache." She touches her forehead with her palm.

"How come?"

"Too much caffeine. I probably won't be able to sleep tonight."

"What happened to your thumb?"

"I cut it—I told you that."

Minho takes her hand and puts it on his knee. "Going to be all right?"

"For sure."

"Mina's wondering why she can't get ahold of you. She said your phone's never on."

"Mina said that?"

"Yeah."

"Which means Mina's the only one trying to get ahold of me."

"No, I sent you a text a while ago." She takes his hand and holds it tight. "Two of them in fact."

"Good for you!"

He smiles. "Did something happen? It's kind of late, isn't it?"

"My phone's not working."

He nods.

"My ex came to my place."

He nods.

"I got into a fight with my teacher at cram school and had to leave class."

He nods.

"I bought a new bag."

He nods.

"Hey, Minho."

He nods.

"Stop messing around and answer me. Minho…you there?"

"I'm listening."

"I've been wanting to see you. Okay?"

Minho nods. She gives him a light smack on the head and scoots out of reach. He makes a face. Giggling, she crushes out her cigarette underfoot and sits back down next to him. He pulls her close again.

"I'm starting to have some regrets about my life. I think I need to make some changes."

He nods.

"Enough nodding. Let's hear some suggestions. You must have *something* to say."

He remains silent, his expression grave.

"What's on your mind?"

"Nothing at all."

"Hey."

"If you want to do something different, then do it. Whatever you want."

"Really? I was thinking the exact same thing. The problem is, my head is killing me. I keep getting hassled—who needs it. It all gives me headaches. I feel like something's going to happen, something big. Killing that kitten wasn't much of anything. This is going to be more serious. Really serious. It's going to happen, I feel it. But—do you think so? Do you think I could? Well, the answer is yes, I can. I can do it. Yeah. I know I can. What do you think? Yeah, I could do it. I could do it, yes I could. I could do it. Crystal could do it. I could do it. I know I could. But really? Really? What do you think? I want to know what you think. It's important. Really important, especially today. So please, listen to me." She lights a fresh cigarette.

"I'm listening."

"Do you believe me?"

"What do you mean?"

"Do you believe me in the truest sense of the word."

"Yes, I do."

"Do you think I could do a good job of it?"

He looks at her and smiles. "I believe in you. Whatever you do, whatever..."

"But how can you? How? Don't you have to know me better first?"

"I read somewhere that if you know someone, then you can't trust him. I don't know you that well, and that's how I can believe in you."

Crystal looks at him and sighs. Then she stubs out her

cigarette. "Yeah, well, I knew you'd say that. I don't expect much from people. Maybe just a little bit of faith in me. And I don't need much in the way of conversation as long as it's warm and honest. But no one talks with me like that. Everybody rejects me. Every…single…person. They do. I know they do." She nods several times in a row. "What do you think?"

"About what?"

"About this. This." She points to the ground. "This. Life."

"You live on, even if it sucks—what else?"

"It's nice that you're so straightforward."

"You are too. Aren't you? You seem like it."

"Yeah, Minho, you're right. And that's why I'm going crazy. It's so annoying. Why is everything in the world so complicated? Why can't it be simple? I'm simple. You're simple. But this world is complicated. Nothing makes sense. All I did was point out a mistake my instructor made, but she got all pissed off and insisted she was right. She was wrong, obviously. I just can't figure that out. Was it pride? Embarrassment? I don't know, but is pride more important than being correct? What the hell? It's ridiculous. How could pride be so important? If she'd been right, then she could be proud, like, automatically. It wouldn't have had to be so complicated. I *just* don't get it. She flipped out. I couldn't put up with it. I took off. I didn't want to keep arguing with her. Hey, why are you laughing?"

"So cute."

"What is?"

"You are."

"Who, me? Cute? Seriously?"

With a smile, Minho nods.

"Really? You're calling me cute? You think I'm cute. So,

you are saying I am cute." Looking up at the sky, she's gets lost in thought, but the next moment she grins. "Wow. I get it. Sure. Great. Yeah, great. Great. Right? It's great that I'm cute. It's great, isn't it? Right?" She pushes his shoulder, wanting to hear it from him.

"Yeah, you're cute."

"How so? In what way? What's so cute about me? Why am I cute?"

"You're different and you're just…cute, that's all."

"So, it's funny?"

"What is?"

"What I'm saying is funny to you?"

"No, not at all."

She springs up from the bench and paces back and forth in front of him. "I really don't like the situation I'm in now—I don't like anything about it," she says, making circles in the air with her finger. "We talk as if I'm water and you're oil. It's been like that from the start. I'm dead serious, but nobody ever takes me seriously. Nobody. Why is that? Why! Why! Why! I don't understand it. I really don't. Minho…I can't take it anymore."

Silence from Minho.

"I'm serious. It's hard for me. If this keeps up…if this keeps up to the end…"

Silence.

"If this keeps up to the end! If this keeps up to the end!"

"You know what the problem is?"

She looks at him.

"You're talking in circles. What's your point?"

"Oh fuck!" she screams. "I'm embarrassed. Don't you see? I'm embarrassed!"

"So tell me," he says in a voice as soft as whipped cream.

"I'll listen, I promise." Hearing that voice leaves her giddy.

"What I'm trying to say... No, I can't. Why can't I just say it! All right, here it is: I'm going to kill another kitten."

"Why?"

"Because nobody listens to me."

Minho looks off into space, nodding.

"You think I'm joking?"

"No."

"Then what?"

Minho looks right at her. "Kill it then," he says in a clipped voice. "Go ahead and kill it, Crystal."

She cackles. "Now I know why Mina doesn't call you *Oppa*. You're not respectable enough to be called a big brother, which is what I like about you. It's what I've liked about you from the start."

Minho laughs, "Stuff like that's not important now."

"Then what is?"

"Following through. Coming up with a perfect plan. Getting rid of your fear."

She nods.

"How are you going to do it? What are you going to do it with? Sixty-five percent of murders in P City involve a knife. It's the most common way, always has been. It's messy but sure. And the rush you'd get when you were doing it would be the best. Besides, knives are easy to buy and no one would suspect you. The other thirty-five percent are beatings, like with a hammer or a baseball bat. Strangling with a chain or something. Throwing someone into the ocean, setting him on fire, beating him to death with your hands, shooting..."

"A knife—I think a knife is best."

"You know how to handle a knife?"

She nods.

"Then you're all set. But killing's not easy. Are you ready for this?"

She nods. "But what if she resists? Meows or something."

"Meows?"

She shrugs. He shrugs.

"Who are you thinking of, anyway?"

"Your sister."

"Really?"

"With a knife."

"You sure you want to *kill* her?"

"What do you think?"

Minho gets lost in thought.

"That flower scent, it's too much."

"Excuse me?"

"Never mind, nothing. What do you think?"

He gives it some more thought, and then, with a nervous giggle, "I'm not sure."

"Why not?"

"I'm coming up blank. But it's going to cause problems, you know."

"It's all because of those lilacs…but so…" She turns to Minho and smiles. The smile twists into a sneer. "Well, why didn't *I* think of it. Yes, indeed, causing problems…but then—you never really like to stake a position, do you?"

"Do you? Aren't you the same?"

"Nope. I've always been a deep thinker."

Now it's Minho who sneers at Crystal.

"You hate your sister, don't you?"

"Why would I hate my sister?"

"Then you love her?"

He nods.

"If you love your sister, then you should say I shouldn't

do it. I'm talking about killing your sister."

Silence.

"I'm done with Mina."

"I'm…"

"You can never be done with Mina—is that what you were going to say?"

"Frankly…" He looks at Crystal and hesitates.

"It's all right, you can tell me. It's okay."

"Frankly, I don't really believe what you're saying."

"What's that supposed to mean? You think I'm joking?"

He nods.

"You mean all of it? Everything?"

He nods.

"Why? How come? Tell me why."

"It's hard to explain."

"I can do it… It's because of that pink Dumbo T-shirt!" Her tone grows sharper. "That's why you think I'm cute. That's why you don't believe me." She frowns. Lowering her head and burying it in her hands, she starts swaying. A faint but piercing moan escapes her palms. Minho gets up and pulls her close. Crystal quiets.

"I wanted to really be serious today. But you aren't taking me seriously. But then if you did I guess I wouldn't talk so seriously. And if you had tried to be serious, I'd probably have joked around and tried to avoid the subject, too. I guess that's our relationship. You don't care no matter what I do, because you don't take me seriously."

She looks at him, wounded. He cups her face in his hands and tries to kiss her. She pushes him away.

"Minho! You're not listening to me! You're not! Nobody listens! Nobody! This shows what my friends think of me. Congratulations, Crystal!" Triumphantly she extends her arms skyward. "Thank you!" she screams. "It's heavenly, that black locust smell!"

Stunned, Minho returns to the bench and sits, down-trodden. He takes a cigarette from Crystal's bag and lights it. She returns to the bench as well, takes his cigarette, and lights one of her own from it.

"Sorry. Look, Crystal, I'm…"

"It's okay, there's nothing to be sorry about. I'm not asking you to apologize. I like this side of you. Really. It's true. You're such a kind guy—why didn't I notice that till now? Of all the guys I've known you're the best. I wish I'd realized it earlier. I should've gotten to know you way back when. Too bad!"

"Hey, Crystal. You keep yelling and somebody is going to report us."

She sighs then continues in a soft, poised tone. "Lately I'm always thinking about what I need to do to make you take me seriously."

"I *do* take you seriously."

"Oh, come on."

"I never talk this much with other girls."

"Who've you been dating, deaf-mutes?"

He bursts into laughter.

"Be honest. Isn't it a problem that I'm Mina's friend?"

"Why do you think like that?"

"Why do I think it's a problem? I admit it, it's my problem, not yours. It's all mine. It's my problem that I get so worked up, too. I wonder if I'm getting delusional. I'm cold."

Minho peels off his hoodie and hands it to her. She puts it on. Arms crossed, he starts shivering. She laughs. "You want it back?" He shakes his head, resolute.

"No, you keep it." She takes something from her bag. A

piece of paper folded four times. She unfolds it and says:

"It's Cesare Lombroso's theories on the physiognomy of a born criminal. Here we go: Assassins have protruding chins, broad cheekbones, dark, thick hair, sparse beards, and pallid faces.

"Assaulters have round skulls and long hands; narrow foreheads are rare.

"Rapists have short hands and small...well, you know... and narrow foreheads. The great majority have light-colored hair and abnormalities of either the genitals or the nose.

"Strong-arm robbers, similar to thieves, have anomalies in skull size along with dark hair and scanty beards.

"Arsonists have small, narrow heads and weigh less than average.

"Swindlers have broad chins and prominent cheekbones, are overweight, and have pale, hardened faces.

"Pickpockets are tall with long hands, black hair, and sparse beards.

"Well," she says, "what do you think?"

"Hmm?" says Minho, a bit dazed. "About what?"

"He says rapists have short hands. What does *that* mean? That the fingers are short? The palms? Or does he mean stubby wrists?"

"He's talking about the whole hand. Like this." Minho displays his arm. "Short hand—see?"

"Really? And swindlers have broad chins?" She holds her hands next to her face to demonstrate. "And prominent cheekbones?" She rests her hands against her cheekbones. "Overweight... With pale faces..." She cups her face. "...and hardened expressions." She puts on a stern look. "Wow, it's not easy to look like a swindler."

"I guess not. Hey, give me another smoke. Wow, it's chilly."

"Mmm. Here you go. You know...I've been thinking. There are too many flowering trees around here. I always feel like I'm suffocating."

"Really?" Minho places a hand on her chest. "You've still got a heartbeat."

She removes his hand and places it on his own chest, then takes a drag off his cigarette.

"They don't say anything here if you smoke? Where I live they don't joke around."

"Nobody's ever said anything to me."

"Cool... You live in a nice place."

"Where'd you get that anyway?"

"I told you—it's from Cesare Lombroso's *Criminal Man*. God, his name is hard to pronounce."

"So what are you doing with it?"

"I like it. I saw an excerpt in my social studies workbook. It's something else, isn't it? I'm trying to memorize it."

"Sure, why not."

She gets up. "I've got to go."

"I'll walk with you."

"You don't have to."

"What's wrong? You mad?"

"No." She lowers her head, whimpering.

"Crystal, what's the matter? Are you crying?"

"Yeah. I'm crying. I... All the stupid things that happened today. I...I want to kill all the people I ran into today. But that's a lot of people. Still, I...I'd do it. Yeah, it wouldn't take long. And then, and then, hey Minho—when it's all over, let's go to Sunday brunch at a hotel. I've been craving stuff that's super fresh. I need something yummy. Homemade bread and a quiche loaded with bacon and cheese. Nice fat rolls of sushi, tofu salad with ginger dressing. I need food that's expensive and makes your mouth water. Summer's coming. Spring is dead. This spring we're having now, it's never coming back. I'm going to erase everything. I hate summer. I want to be rid of it. I wish half the people in the world would just disappear. I hope the Amazon rain forest grows lush again. I hope nature recovers and stars fill the night sky. No more wars and no more terror anywhere on the globe, no more environmental degradation, no more endangering polar bears. Maybe I should work for the U.N. so I can help. Listen to me. I'm begging you. *Really* listen. In one minute, no, in thirty seconds I'll be gone. I won't be here. I'll have erased everything from my mind. That's the way it goes. I'll forget everything. There's not much time left now. I'll wipe it out. I'll wipe it all out. I don't like all these complications. So I'm getting rid of everything. The thing is, I…I…I love you. Don't you know that? How can I get that across to you? I don't like confusion, and yet I'm so confused. My heart's beating. I'm such a normal girl, and yet the world is stickier and grosser than a spiderweb—why is that? Will you *please* try to understand me? If you can understand me, my heart and my soul, you can eat worms, mosquitos, roaches, whatever, and then you can kiss me. And I'll kiss you. I give you permission. You're perfect for me, *Oppa*. And no one else, remember that."

"Okay, I just feasted on all of it," Minho says, then he kisses her.

Eying him, she wipes her mouth with the back of her hand. "All right. I know what's on your mind. I'm disappointed in you. But I can't help it, because I love you. You don't understand. You don't look at me the same way you look at people who are like *you*. Because of you my heart is crumbling. Why can't you feel it? I want to cry. I feel like killing myself."

Minho pleads. He says he loves her. He says not to cry and not to kill herself.

"I won't ever kill myself. Why would I want to do that? I'll never, ever kill myself."

And they kiss again.

DAWN AT THE SUPERSTORE

Her head is full of voices. They continue even when she turns off the music. Even if she takes off her headphones. There are at least five of them. Each jabbering away in a different language. One screams "Banana!" in English. Another says, "The kettle is hot" in Chinese. Another says, "It's in the drawer" in Korean. One of them calls her by name—Crystal. That voice is despicably sweet. "You can run," it says to her. "And you can crawl. But you don't need to be a different person."

She's still wide awake.

Several times during the night she's sat up in bed, only to fall back again. The time has passed slowly, until she arrives at an awkward decision point: either do something or keep trying to fall asleep. It's the dead of night, and nothing, absolutely nothing is happening, and she's the only one who's awake. Her uneasiness continues: Does she feel like crying, or does she feel like laughing? Remembering yesterday, she thinks of how much she has done and concludes that there's nothing more to be done. Except to get some sleep. Everything happened yesterday. A new bright morning is approaching. But she stays awake. The more time that passes, the clearer her mind. She scowls, buries her face in her pillow, and then rubs it slowly against the pillow, moaning. Several brief but deep fits of sleep later, she gives up. She checks the time: 3:47. She goes out to the living room, paces back and forth a few times, then goes into the bathroom and turns on the shower.

Cold water pours over her chest. Instantly she cringes, before ducking her head into the stream until her limp, sodden hair clings to her face. She finds the shampoo and lathers until her hair is white with foam. She looks grave and pensive, but she's not really thinking about much of anything. Afterward she moves busily through the unlit rooms, but quietly enough to not wake her parents. In her room she packs her new messenger bag, in the bathroom she blow-dries her hair. Then back in her room she gets dressed; she goes to the kitchen for a drink of water. Back in the bathroom she combs and applies conditioner to her hair. In her room she sprays perfume, and then she takes her bag to the entryway and sets it down. She sits on the sofa and thinks for a moment, considering the phone. She flips the TV on and then off. She picks up the phone and puts it back down. She retrieves her bag from the entryway, takes it to her room, empties it, and sorts through the contents. Back into the bag go her notebooks, pencil case, cigarettes, and MP3 player, and on top she adds her school uniform. She turns on her computer and checks social media, blogs, and email. Her news feed carries a headline in boldface: "High School Girls Having Group Sex." She checks the weather. Then she logs onto her favorite sites, typing in her IDs, her passwords. She prints out a page, looks it over, nods, then folds it in half, sticks it in one of the notebooks, and adds the notebook to her bag. One last check of the contents and she zips the bag shut. Turning off the light, she leaves; the door to her room stays open. She crosses the living room to shut the bathroom door, puts on her shoes in the entryway, and surveys the apartment before leaving.

As soon as she's outside, a vacant taxi appears. She hails it and the taxi pulls up in front of her. She tells the driver where she wants to go, and he asks if she minds if he smokes. She nods—fine. He rolls down his window and lights up. A cold wind blows. The streets are dark and deserted, but the distant skies are brightening. Fretfully she clenches her fists. She watches anxiously as the streets slowly recover their distinctive colors with the gradually lightening sky. The news comes on over the radio. The driver curses the government. Crystal looks back out the window. The driver stubs out his cigarette. More news: politics, the weather, the economy. She feels anger rising inside her and tries not to let it show. A solitary, brightly lit superstore appears in the distance.

"Go straight and drop me off up there, please," she says, pointing to the mart.

The double glass doors to the store lurch open as she approaches. She marches straight through. Very few customers at this hour, all of their faces wooden with fatigue. A jaunty hit song from last winter—or was it last fall?—plays. She starts looking around. There are Barbies, DVDs, pet food, underwear, socks, Harry Potter action figures. Turning left from an aisle of snow-white washing machines, she pauses at the kitchenware section and lingers before a display of translucent dishes with bright orange designs. And then, looking serious, she surveys several varieties of tea cups. She tries out cutting boards by tapping them with a knuckle, then cuts through the kitchen knife display to the grocery section. She takes a bar of chocolate and wanders a bit before heading to the fruit. Picking up a shopping basket from a pile next to a crate of apples, she drops the chocolate bar into it. She carefully examines the selection of instant noodle soup, then moves on to a display of bottled water, adding a bottle to her basket. She passes down the rice aisle and through the bakery, arriving at the oils and spices. She picks up various brands of salad dressing, one at a time, then returns them to the shelf. Reversing direction and retracing her route, she comes across bamboo salt and puts a container in her basket. Now she's back to the kitchenware. She takes a silver lemon squeezer and examines it for some time, compares it with a corkscrew, and then returns both items to their places. She checks the ladles, examines a variety of can openers. On a top shelf wire scrubbers are on sale; open-mouthed she admires the intricate coils. Beyond the can openers she passes metal measuring cups, tongs, kitchen shears, and barbecue forks; she comes to a stop before the kitchen knives.

There's a plentiful array. Packaged neatly in transparent plastic bearing a photo of the knife and instructions, the knives are numerous, their uses various—they are shiny and easy to handle. The knives for chopping onions have a photo of onions on the package; paring knives have a photo of an orange or an apple; vegetable knives have a photo of a cucumber or celery stalk. Butcher knives have a photo of beef, fillet knives a photo of fresh fish. There are also sushi knives. There are expensive knives and some knives on sale, priced more reasonably. There are imported knives and domestic ones, knives with blunt tips and pointed ones. There are generic knives bearing the superstore brand name. She hesitates— which one to choose, an import or a domestic?—then reaches for an onion knife. The next moment everything has turned black and white. Only the numerous knives in their splendid colors stand out to her. Startled, she pulls her hand back. The background returns to its normal colors. After a cautious look around she ventures a hand toward a sushi knife. Again:

everything turns black and white. All the knives reach for her. Crystal paws at the air, takes hold of one. It grabs her hand tight. There is no longer anything else, only blinding white space. A single melody fills the air. All of the hands applaud her, and she kisses one of them. She curtsies, turning in a perfect circle. The hands stroke, grab, and grope her. An enchanted smile blossoms on her face. The hands take her by the neck and press her down toward the shelving. What now? Still she manages to keep smiling.

And then she screams.

She's backed into a shelf of plastic cups and they tumble down on her. Collecting herself, she replaces the cups. She looks into her basket and finds two knives—a large German-made one with a cool gleam and sharp point, wrapped in red plastic but without a photo, and a butcher knife with a picture of raw beef. She looks around. Everything has returned to its original color, but there's a pale shine. She tries reaching for a grill fork. Nothing happens. *Hmm, too bad.* Quickly she leaves. Passing by the stacking storage cubes, she sees clothespins and clotheslines and adds a pack of each to her basket. She stops by the bakery, has three bites of a bread sample, and heads for the checkout lines.

Only two of the checkout lanes are open. Waiting in front of her are a couple and a middle-aged woman with dark circles under her eyes who looks sleep-deprived. Crystal places her items on the counter. The cashier looks to be in her early thirties. She greets Crystal in a mechanical voice and scans the items without looking at her, saying the prices out loud. Everyone looks tired. But not Crystal. She pays, then looks back at the mounds of merchandise in the white, windowless interior. Knotting her plastic bag, she places it in her messenger bag. Through the glass doors at the entrance she sees the streets brightening in the blue light of morning. She approaches the doors and they slide open for her. Waiting for a taxi to pass, she puts her headphones back on and lights a cigarette. People stare at her. She tilts her head up and back toward the sky, opens her mouth wide, and blows out smoke. The smoke vanishes into the dawn air. She takes her hand from her pocket and checks her watch: 5:53. She watches the brightening sky with a doomed expression. Crushing out her cigarette, she hails a cab and it comes to a stop.

"Go straight and drop me off up there, please."

She passes through the school gate, crosses the playground, and enters the building. There isn't a soul around. The hallway is dark and quiet and there's a touch of warmth to the air. A primeval sweetness, identical to that of the Jell-O in her closet, clings to her every cell, giving her the thrilling sensation of wanting to cut her inner thigh with a knife. She goes into her homeroom, not bothering to turn on the lights. She sits at her seat, takes the notebooks from her messenger bag, and makes sure the folded piece of paper is still there. She puts the paper in her desk drawer, then takes her school uniform from the bag and places it on the desk. She checks the plastic bag, reties it, then takes it to her locker at the back of the room. She opens the locker, checks the class schedule taped inside, takes the textbooks she needs, and leaves her messenger bag. Locking the locker, she returns to her desk, picks up the uniform, and sets down the books in its place. She leaves for the bathroom and returns shortly in her neat uniform. Unlocking the locker, she retrieves her bag, puts her street clothes inside, then returns the bag to the locker. Locking it, she returns to her desk. She straightens her back and does a series of stretches. She puts on her headphones and presses Play. She takes one of her workbooks from the desk drawer. Then, pencil in hand, she looks down at it.

Suddenly she looks up—sunlight dazzles outside the window. Kids are all around her. She checks the clock on the back wall. She's closed her workbook, leaned back in her chair, and is yawning when Jina pokes her in the back. Crystal jumps to her feet.

"You okay? You were working like crazy on those problems."

"What? When do I ever do that?"

"You had a mad gleam in your eye."

"Oh—so, not being able to sleep equals mad gleam?"

"You were up all night studying?"

"No, I don't study at night," says Crystal, looking at Jina. "All kinds of stuff happened. Hey, I'm starved. Let's go get something to eat."

At the snack bar she picks out a curry croquette and a carton of banana milk, while Jina, always conscious of her diet, opts for calorie-free organic green tea. They find a bench.

"Hey, Jina, can I make a call on your phone?"

Jina hands it to her. "Where's yours?"

"It's not working… Uh, hello? Mom? It's Crystal. Mom, did you happen to get a call from cram school? Really? That's strange. Ah no, nothing. Hmm? No, I had a few things to do, so I left early. Mmm, I had some pastries. No, I'm okay. By the way, Mom, is it okay if I get the new phone tomorrow? I'm feeling kind of tired—is it all right if I skip cram school tonight, just this once? Oh, I might just have a touch of the flu. And my back's sore. And I'd love some sushi. Yeah, sushi! All right, sushi! Mmm, let's ask Dad too. Let's do that. Can you? When do you think you'll be home? I see. Yeah. Love you too. Bye."

"You okay, Crystal? You got the flu?"

"No." She shakes her head, then mumbles: "Cellphone, tomorrow. Cram school, tomorrow. Sushi, tomorrow. Mom, tomorrow. Today. Today. Yeah, let's do it."

"What?"

"Never mind. Just talking to myself. Everything's fine. All good."

Stuffing the rest of her croquette in her mouth, she wipes the grease from her lips and drains what's left in her carton of milk.

"Hey, Jina."

"Mmm?"

"All done?"

"I'm gonna finish my tea inside."

"Sure, sounds good, let's go. But hey, first, how about once around the field? I need a walk. My head's spinning. Yeah, some air. Actually, forget it, I don't. Let's just go in."

"Huh?"

"Let's hurry back."

Jina nods. Crystal locks arms with her. Jina blocks the sun with her other hand.

"By the way…is Mina okay?"

"Sure. She transferred, you know."

"Really? You saw her? How is she? Why'd she transfer?"

"Well, I've been wondering myself. Why would she want to do that? I should have asked her."

"You saw her recently?"

Crystal nods.

"How was she?"

Crystal gives Jina a blank look.

"Tell me."

Frowning, Crystal shakes her head.

"Okay, I get it...."

"No, actually—"

"Crystal, if it's that tough you don't have to say anything. I get it. Really, I do."

Nodding, Crystal gazes out the window. Jina looks out as well. Crystal presses her nose to the glass, desperately looking at something outside.

"Crystal, what are you looking at?"

"That tree...that tree..."

"That tree?"

"...I can see it growing."

"Duh! That's what living things do."

"What a great tree. That's a great tree all right. Wow!"

Jina is confused. A bell rings—ten minutes until the first class. Crystal and Jina go back to their classroom and take their seats.

"Watch out!" a voice booms. "Inspection of personal belongings!"

There's a brief silence, followed immediately by a clamor of yells, curses, and sighs from all directions.

"Downstairs must've been raided already."

Eyes wide, Crystal chews on her thumbnail. Suppressing her shock and fear, she tells herself to focus and looks back at her locker. Her heart is pounding. She tries to relax by breathing deeply but it doesn't work. Pen held tight in one hand, she repeatedly folds and unfolds a page in her textbook.

"When's ours?"

"Start of class."

"You've gotta be kidding me!"

"Fuck, how am I going to hide this CD?"

"Just erase it. Wipe it clean."

"No—I want to back it up first!"

The boys check their stacks of CDs, their external hard drives, their cellphones. Girls gather their cigarettes to hide in the toilet tanks.

Amid the chaos of the classroom Crystal quietly flips through her textbook.

Someone puts a hand on her shoulder. "Anything you need to get rid of?"

"Nope."

"Good for you."

In no time the bell rings. Crystal takes the Band-Aid off her thumb and worries the tip with her teeth while tapping on her desk with her other hand. Blood oozes from the thumb. She wipes it on her skirt. Just as she's rising from her seat, the teacher opens their classroom door. Crystal sits back down. She begins gnawing at her thumb again. Blood continues to ooze, slowly and steadily. With a wide smile the teacher announces the inspection. The students respond with grumbles. Crystal looks at her bleeding thumb, then rubs it with her forefinger until the thumb is covered in blood. Again she chews the thumb. She feels a bone-deep pain and trembles all over. She licks her bloody lips. She rests the thumb on her desk and watches the blood ooze from it until there's a stream of red. Someone points to her thumb with a look of shock. Several kids turn toward Crystal. Crystal looks up, sees the other kids, looks down to check that the thumb is still bleeding, slowly raises her hand, and calls out to the teacher.

"Crystal, is something the matter?"

Crystal extends the thumb, blood now pouring from it. The teacher startles. By way of explanation Crystal mimics cutting paper with a knife.

"Get to the nurse's office, now."

There's a buzz among the kids. Crystal gets up and walks

toward the door at the rear of the classroom. Curious eyes follow her. She takes one step, two steps, and at the third she collapses, limp, to the floor. Students scream and Jina rushes to her side. The teacher comes over. Somebody calls out her name. Crystal opens her eyes, but for a moment they don't move or react. The floor is slick with blood from her thumb. Jina shakes her shoulder, and Crystal slowly sits up. Her face betrays no emotion, but she's making an effort to smile, nodding and waving her hand.

"I'm okay." From her constricted throat it sounds like a nail scratching a steel plate. "I'm all right, ma'am. I'll go to the nurse's office."

"Are you all right going by yourself?"

"Yes."

Jina takes her arm.

"It's okay. I can manage."

"No, I'm going with you. You're too pale." Jina points to a mirror next to the lockers. "Just look at yourself."

Leaning against Jina, Crystal lowers her head to avoid looking in the mirror.

The hallways are still. Jina keeps asking Crystal if she's all right, and Crystal keeps shaking her head no. The nurse's office comes into view, the bright white walls and the white cotton sheets visible through the half-open door. The air in the empty hallway smells of rubbing alcohol and medication. Crystal perches on a bed, nervously jiggling her leg. Jina looks around the office curiously. Crystal gets back up and begins pacing.

"Who's there?" comes a voice.

"I cut my thumb. Can I have a Band-Aid, please?"

The nurse comes in. "Let's have a look."

Crystal extends her thumb. The nurse moves in close to

examine it. She holds her breath; the man's moisturizer has an overpowering smell.

He looks her in the eye. "It doesn't look like a cut to me."

Crystal puts the hand behind her back. He shakes his head.

"Let's start with some disinfectant. You might feel a little sting, all right?" With a moistened cotton ball he carefully wipes the wound until the torn skin is clearly visible. "This isn't a cut. Is it a dog bite? What happened?"

"No. No, it's not."

"Are you sure? If it's a dog bite, then…"

"Yes, I'm sure."

Jina watches them, confused.

"It was a knife, really. Not a dog. Please. It's an old knife and it's pretty dull. I'm sorry but I need to get back to class, so could we hurry and…" She checks the clock on the wall. The nurse looks too.

"Oh well, all right."

He takes a Band-Aid from a drawer and bandages her thumb, his eyes continuing to search her. Crystal tries to keep her expression calm. He gives her some extra Band-Aids.

"They're waterproof, so don't worry about water touching them. And they've got a little bit of disinfectant added. Fancy, see?"

She nods.

"Okay, let's get you to class. When school's over, come on back so we can disinfect it again. Got it?"

She nods.

"All right, run along then."

The girls bow politely and leave. Crystal starts up the stairs.

"Hey, what are you doing? We need to go down."

"I'm going to the teachers' office."

"Why? And why was the nurse saying your cut wasn't from a knife? And why didn't you tell him you fainted?"

Crystal stops and glares at her. Shaking her head in exasperation, she starts up the steps again. The next moment she's stopped and leaning against the railing, holding her forehead and moaning.

Jina shouts, "Crystal, are you all right?"

Crystal rushes back downstairs. Jina watches, perplexed. Crystal grabs Jina's wrist and then rushes back up the stairs—Jina is being hauled along before she knows it's happening. Her shoes come off.

"Hey, my shoes!"

"Right, your shoes—not my shoes."

Jina knocks Crystal's hand away and stops. Crystal grabs her by the neck. Jina chokes and flails her hands at the air. Holding tight to her neck, Crystal climbs the remaining stairs. At the top she releases Jina, who breathes heavily, her panting echoing in the quiet hallway.

"Shut up. Don't say anything. Wait here." Crystal pulls one of Jina's ears. Face stiff from fright, Jina pushes her away. A smile blossoms on Crystal's face. "Wait here."

Crystal walks through the teachers' room, bowing to several teachers. Her homeroom teacher, chin propped up on her palm, is focused on a computer.

"May I leave early?"

The teacher breaks her gaze from the monitor and regards Crystal. She sees a student with a pale face holding tight to her thumb and trembling.

"What's the matter? Aren't you feeling well? Here, sit."

"I think I have a cold," says Crystal.

The teacher feels her forehead, "Well maybe you do.

Feels like you have a touch of fever."

"Yes."

"Mmm…can you hang on a bit longer? Just till the end of morning classes?"

Silence.

"No? What happened to your thumb?"

"I cut it with a knife. I guess I was spacing out because of the fever." She gives the teacher a feeble smile.

The teacher gazes at her, deep in thought. Silence. And then, with a pat on her shoulder, the teacher grins. "Well, if you're sick you're sick, not much we can do." The teacher begins to fill out an early-dismissal pass, then pauses, looking at Crystal, "Didn't you leave early last Monday?"

"No," says Crystal, a slight edge to her tone.

"Guess I'm confusing you with someone else. This is your first early dismissal of the term?"

"Yes."

"Okay." Handing Crystal the pass, the teacher crosses her legs. "All right, you can go now. Get yourself some rest and see you tomorrow."

Pass in hand, Crystal stands with a bright smile.

"By the way, how is the prep for the field trip going?"

"Oh gosh, how would I know? You should ask the class monitor…" Crystal bows to her, grinning.

The teacher fixes her with a stare as Crystal makes a show of hobbling to the door.

Carefully she opens the classroom door. All eyes turn to her. She sees Jina—*I knew she wouldn't actually wait!* Head down, Jina is looking at her notebook. Crystal approaches and places a hand on her shoulder. Jina looks up. Crystal's smiling from ear to ear. Her lips are tense and trembling, but she holds the smile. Jina turns away. With a sigh Crystal takes her hand off of Jina's shoulder and walks over to the teacher.

"Sorry you're not feeling well," says the teacher, looking at Crystal's pass.

Eyes down, Crystal goes to her desk and gathers her things. Then she goes to her locker, opens it, takes out her messenger bag, and puts it on the floor. Into the locker go her textbooks, into her bag go her pencil case and workbooks. She turns and glances at the teacher. She's writing something on the whiteboard, the dry-erase marker squeaking. Closing her bag and locking her locker, Crystal quietly heads for the rear door. Before she gets there, her eyes meet Jina's. Crystal isn't smiling anymore. Jina watches her as Crystal walks the rest of the way to the door. Crystal, eyes still on Jina, bangs her head against the door. Jina bursts out laughing and the next moment turns back to the class. Crystal quietly opens and then shuts the door behind her. Through a window into the next classroom she sees that the inspection is nearly done. Off she runs.

AT MINA'S

"*Oppa*, where are you? Can you come over?

"No? Why not?

"Come to me, please.

"Somebody out there come to me.

"Somebody out there come to me.

"Somebody out there come to me.

"Or I'll kill all of you.

"Or I'll kill all of you."

Crystal smiles.

"Or I'll kill all of you."

Pointing at the pedestrians outside the phone booth, she says, "You. Every last one of you. I'll kill you.

"I'll kill every last one of you.

"I haven't figured out how just yet," she shouts into the phone. "But I will."

Suddenly she remembers the folded sheet of paper in her notebook. "I don't know. I don't know. I just don't. Will someone please come to me? Please?

"I can't call everybody. Someone just come. Then I'll feel better." She throws the receiver and squats, her face crinkling. Rubbing her eyes with the backs of her hands, she heaves a faint sigh. When she removes her hands, her eyes moisten again. The morning sun is heating to a midsummer sizzle and the phone booth is suffocating. She looks out blankly and her eyes meet those of a man walking by. She stands and picks up the receiver.

"Come to me...I can't do anything...but that doesn't make me a failure."

She emerges from the phone booth and walks away, wondering where to go. It's still early and most of the shops aren't open yet. She thinks of a few places to go, but she shrugs them off. She checks the time. She's hungry. She decides she wants breakfast but keeps walking. She's famished. Her legs are about to buckle. Her toes are stiff and hot and each leg feels like a thick phone book. She's dizzy. And sweating. She enters a Starbucks. Drip coffee and tuna wrap in hand, she goes into the bathroom. She changes from her school uniform back into her street clothes, applies powder and lip gloss, and looks at herself in the mirror. She leaves the bathroom and goes into the smoking area. The people give her looks: *that girl seems awfully young to be smoking.* She stuffs the tuna wrap in her mouth and drinks her coffee. And then she lights up. She looks around. Checks the time. Gazes vacantly through the glass partition as she smokes. Stubs out her cigarette and rises. Her messenger bag drops to the floor. Eyes are on her. Shrugging, she shoulders the bag, and leaves to find another phone booth.

"Who is it?" she hears Minho shout. It's impossible to hear with all the noise in the background.

Blocking her other ear, she shouts back, "Where are you? Are you at school?"

"Crystal? Is that you?"

"Yeah."

"Where are you? At school?"

"No."

"You're skipping?"

"No, I took an early dismissal."

"How come? Are you sick?"

"What?"

"I said, are you sick!"

"No, I'm okay!"

"You don't sound okay!"

"I'm just a little tired."

"What? I can't hear you!"

"I said I'm a bit tired!"

"Then go home and get some sleep."

"No, I'm going to your place."

"Really? I think Mina left for school."

"But she'll be home soon?"

"Huh?"

"Yeah!"

"What?"

"I didn't say anything."

"Uh…sorry…hang on…can you hear me now?"

"Wow. How'd you do that?"

"I came outside."

"Well, it worked."

"So, why do you want to go to my place?"

"Just because."

"You know, I didn't tell Mina I saw you yesterday."

"How come?"

"Should I have told her?"

"No, it's good you didn't. When are you getting home?"

"Not till late."

"Okay."

"Let's try to meet up later."

"I love you!" Crystal shouts.

No response.

"Why aren't you saying anything?"

"I'm listening."

"I know you don't love me, but I love you."

"Crystal, you always talk like that…I like you too."

"Look. It's not like I'm asking you to commit, I know you better than that. Anyway, thanks. I don't know…when I think about you, Minho…I get all weepy."

"Are you crying? Hey, Crystal, don't cry."

"I'm not. I'm just saying… Why would I be crying? Minho, by the way…"

"What?"

"I'm out of money. Time's up."

"Okay. Call me later. Let's try to meet up this evening."

"All right, bye."

"Okay, bye."

The moment she hangs up her heart starts drumming; she's getting angry. She thinks, her unfocused eyes boring holes in the distance. Smiling bashfully, she closes her eyes and then opens them. A short time later she does it again. No one notices her. No one knows what she's thinking. That no one is thinking about Crystal right now is her responsibility. But what would responsibility or purpose have to do with anything? Regardless of responsibility, things will happen according to their fate. And they are happening now: fate has arrived. Now a bus arrives. Crystal gets on.

Under the rising heat, the scent of the lilac and black locust blossoms attacks Crystal with a different zing than at night. On this fragrance-smothered path she watches, helpless, as all of her thoughts drift away. Stripped of their shells, they take on a liquid form that flows and ebbs. And the thoughts all gradually ebb and break apart behind her. It's alluring yet risky to try and follow them. Ultimately, she's powerless in their presence, and drifts defenselessly among the flowing thoughts awaiting a respite that doesn't come. She merely drifts, further and further off. Just when she feels like bursting into tears, Madonna's "Vogue" comes through her headphones again. She feels excitement build and has an urge to run into the garden, grab hold of a lilac bush, and dance circles around it. But the garden is for Residents Only. That thought makes her a bit sad, but she concentrates on the music. She turns up the volume and the music comes a step closer. The intro to "Vogue" never fails to pump her up with anticipation, and then out comes Madonna's dreamy, silky pink voice. She's never seen Madonna perform in person but has gotten used to hearing the song everywhere; it has been famous since she was young, but she's only recently been really listening to it, concentrating on it from beginning to end, and now every time she hears it she falls in love with it again. Crystal marvels at Madonna's bravura voice. She also knows all about contemporary Madonna. On the gossip channel she sees Madonna's silky blond hair and porcelain white skin, her mastery of intricate dance steps even though she's over fifty, her explicit allure to her teenage fans onstage. Crystal also knows all about her celebrated filmmaker husband, her infatuation with yoga and kabbalah, her strict ban on her children watching TV, the controversy over her adopting a child from Africa, her writing children's books, her living in London. She knows that Madonna loves to wear long clinging coats but performs just as provocatively as the younger singers, and on MTV Crystal can see her practically anytime. And yet

Madonna's daughter doesn't get to watch her perform on TV. She's arrogant, but for Crystal, Madonna's assortment of contradictions makes sense. They are precisely why Crystal likes her. Her contradictory attitudes come not from some personal defect—the assumption of an ignorant public—but from a core irony of all great people. That irony is a hallmark of a winner, and if you want to win you need to be illogical, powerful, and destructive, and the more of each the better. Crystal wishes to elevate her characteristic incoherency to the lofty plane of Madonna's contradictions, and that's why she admires her.

Everybody knows Madonna. She's as much of a megastar now as she has ever been, but Crystal has never been one of her most devoted fans. Crystal is more familiar with alternative types, witches and outliers—PJ Harvey, Liz Phair, Fiona Apple, Björk. She knows them better, likes them more, and listens to them more often than Madonna. But that isn't a choice of hers, but rather a matter of Mina's influence. But where does one draw the line between her own choices and the influence of others? Don't we all grow within a realm of others' influence? Thin-skinned types fall into despair when they can't escape that realm, but that merely shows us they're short on critical thinking and they've missed the point—how can people like that contribute anything to the world? Can it be possible to make choices in an absence of influence from others? Can we break off from the preferences of those around us and make choices of our own? Is that possible? Is it then possible to act on our own? Of course, our time and space make us into people with different agendas. But that's only a different mix within a fixed makeup. Freedom is nothing but the myth of a bygone romantic era. Crystal doesn't believe that myth. The only freedom she believes in is a place where she can go but others can't. In practice she doesn't believe in such a thing as independence. Rather, hope lies in being fused and buried in a group—a core group. Her credo is that alternative schools, and alternatives in general, are consolation prizes for losers.

It was from Mina's influence that Crystal began listening to music. And Mina began because of the influence of her father. Mina and Minho like the stacks of records and the speakers that fill their father's study with sound. Mina's father listens to the Doors, so Mina does too. Mina didn't need to buy Pink Floyd's albums; her father had them. Mina didn't have to work hard, all she had to do was pick from the selection of books and records and make them her own. Arrayed on one of the shelves in her father's study were some fancy old cameras. The expensive devices were decades old and operated with a cheerful click of the shutter. Back when Crystal was becoming close with Mina she was invited to go with Mina's family to a Eugène Atget exhibit. Once she figured out how to spell the weird name she found online that Atget was a noted French photographer—the god, father, and holy spirit of photography. Putting aside various other temptations she went to the exhibit. It was at a gallery in the ritziest part of the city and was thronged with families who moseyed through with sagacious expressions, taking in the photos from a vanished era. At the entrance was Atget's name, chocolate in color, in a massive but elegant cursive font. Below, in a Korean translation whose attempt to reflect French syntax was a disaster, was an introduction to his life and work. The striking black-and-white photos mounted in high-quality frames were accompanied by elegant labels in cursive French and English and, beneath them, in a clunky Korean font. Crystal tried to seriously understand these elegant artistic artifacts. But how was she to appreciate the deserted streets, buildings, nameless people, and objects, all of them reeking of nostalgia? If she felt anything at all, it was her tired legs. *This is supposed to be impressive?* It was all just a big production for wannabe petit-bourgeois Koreans to feel like their postwar European counterparts.

There are so many books in Mina's father's study. There are classics and inflammatory, provocative books that university students peek at on their laps during classes. Musty-smelling books of literature from postwar South Korea. Sensational books of photos—popular with teenagers—by contemporary American photojournalists. All kinds of books. Books by that damned Jung. Their composition tutor used to marvel at Mina with her refined and old-fashioned cultural tastes, nodding with pleasure at whatever Mina said. Crystal was the one with the powerful, perfectly structured compositions, yet the tutor doted on Mina's clumsy writing. Whenever Crystal spotted the two of them smiling affectionately at each other she would curse the teacher: *Whatever, bitch, you'll be a shit tutor your whole life and then drop dead.* The tutor would loan Mina various books that they would then chat about jubilantly the subsequent week. If Mina name-dropped one of her favorite poets, the tutor would respond with some hard-to-pronounce European or Japanese names and suggest more books. Composition classes with Mina were hell for Crystal. Mina may not have admired Crystal, but during these tutoring sessions Crystal couldn't help but look up to Mina. They were the only times that she couldn't find a way to look down on her, even though she recognized the sessions were a game, albeit an important one she played to win. She tried piling the books the tutor recommended on her desk. But it was bizarre—the more effort she put in, the higher Mina rose and the more she herself sank. *What's the problem?* The question tormented her for hours on end, but the answer never came. Until today.

Fucking idiots, reading useless books, I ought to kill every one of you.

Crystal suddenly understands, deeply, why the first Qin emperor burned the books and buried the scholars. *That's right. Regardless of when, there's always human garbage. I get it. Totally understand. Just think of all the weird books in the world and all the conversations by the weirdos who read them. Workbooks for the university entrance exam are all you need. Burn the rest of them. Thank god the era of the written word is over and it's now the era of images. Thank god we won't even have to lift a finger for all that human trash to get dumped. The adults will eventually get sick and die, it's only natural. The problem is kids like Mina. Why, why, why, why! Why! She stuffs her brain with the same shit and then I do the same! And for what? Garbage! Fucking garbage, all of it!*

The music climbs to its rousing finale; Madonna asks her to dance and sing along. The next moment Crystal has pushed thoughts of Mina aside in favor of Madonna, who is urging her to use her imagination, that's what it's for. She bobs her head, rushing into the lobby of the opulent apartment building. The young security guard in his navy blue uniform acts as if he knows her.

"Have you seen Mina? Is she here?"

He nods and says something she can't make out over the music. She takes off her headphones and everything is suddenly silent. The guard calls Mina's apartment and Crystal shows her face to the intercom's camera. The guard nods, makes a note in the computer, and hands her a visitor's card. She swipes the card at the elevators; the doors of one of them open, and then they close behind her. Pressing one of the buttons, she bows to the guard through the glass door.

The corridor is silent. She presses Mina's doorbell and smiles into the camera. Once inside she sees the long narrow hallway in front of her. The study, bathroom, dining room, and kitchen are to the right. The living room with its chandelier is at the end. Minho and Mina's rooms and their parents' suite with its walk-in closet and bathroom are to the left. In the subdued hallway with its high ceiling are a few small tables, each with an unlit lamp that hasn't been used in ages and is coated with dust. Beneath the pair of windows she can see at the far end of the living room is a large floor lamp made of fiberglass fashioned into an orange peacock. Its detailing is so elaborate it looks like all the peacock has to do is spread its wings and it could fly away. That lamp is always lit, along with the chandelier, and its long, ominous shadow looks like a tail. The sun goes behind a cloud and Crystal notices the unlit hallway is unusually dark—even the light from the peacock seems listless and unsteady. She closes the front door and removes her shoes, then opens her messenger bag. After taking out the plastic bag she tosses the messenger bag on the floor. Perfectly composed, she strides down the hall, opening the plastic bag and looking into each room in turn. The doors to the study and Minho's room are open but no one's inside them. Suddenly, the rooms off the hall are flooded with hazy afternoon sunlight. Mina's not in the bathroom. Drawn across the entry to the dining room are a pair of ivory-colored curtains embroidered with grapevines. She pulls them open. Mina isn't there either. Crtystal comes to the living room. The gray and green colors of downtown are visible through the windows. Looking down, she realizes summer has arrived. She switches off the peacock lamp. The apartment becomes noticeably gloomier. Crystal's shadow blends in with the darkness. She goes into Mina's parents' room and rummages through the clothes in the walk-in closet. Mina's not there. She pokes around the bedroom with its neatly made bed but no Mina. *What am I doing in here?* She leaves, goes to Mina's room, and opens her closet. *Nope.* She returns to Mina's parents' room, passes the walk-in closet, and opens the door to their bathroom.

"Hey, shut the fucking door!" Mina shouts.

Startled, Crystal shuts the door. Then she opens it a crack and says softly, "Sorry."

"I said close the door!"

"All right." She closes it. "Take your time."

Back in the living room she turns the peacock lamp on and then off again before sprawling on the rug. She shakes her head and then scratches it and sighs deeply. She gets up and moves over to the sofa. She takes everything out of the plastic bag and lays it all out on the floor—knives, water bottle, bamboo salt, chocolate, clothesline, and clothespins. She looks blankly out the window, then goes into the study. She connects her MP3 player to the speakers. She turns the knob on the speaker but there's no sound. She turns the volume all the way up. No sound. *Aha.* She plugs in the cord to the speakers and sound explodes like a bomb. Jolted, she unplugs them. Adjusting the volume, she plugs the cord back in again. The song starts from the beginning, and this time Madonna's voice isn't distorted.

Humming, she heads to Mina's room. Rummaging through Mina's backpack, she notices something that leaves her looking around anxiously. But then her eyes land on the desk and she smiles. Grabbing Mina's cellphone, she goes to the kitchen, puts the phone in the sink, and turns on the water.

Then, turning off the faucet, she returns to the living room and unwraps the knives. She sets them on the floor, takes a sip of water, and nibbles on the chocolate. A knife in each hand, she stretches out on the sofa. She lurches, goes over to the TV, and cuts the landline next to it. Heading back to the kitchen with the wireless phone, she passes the intercom. Carefully she turns it off and unplugs the line. Tossing the phone in the sink, she turns on the water again. Now that all the phones are dead, she goes back to the sofa, stretches out, and closes her eyes.

"Hey, what're you doing?" When Crystal opens her eyes she sees Mina looking bewildered as she rubs lotion into her arms. Mina is wearing a pink Hello Kitty bathrobe. Pointing at the bathrobe with the tip of her knife, Crystal says, almost bashfully, "I gave that to you for your birthday."

"What are you doing here?"

"What happened to the music?"

"I turned it off."

"How come?"

"I don't like it."

"Why not?"

"I just don't like it."

Crystal's face hardens.

Mina flinches. "But, you…"

"I asked you why you turned it off. Why can't you give me a real answer? Are you stupid or something? Why did you do that? Why did you turn off the music?"

"Is there something wrong with that?"

"Yes!"

"What?"

"*I* turned it on. I turned on the music."

"Okay, well, then I'm sorry." Reluctantly she looks Crystal up and down. "Go ahead, turn it back on."

Crystal lowers her head and shrugs, then looks up at Mina, satisfied. "Thank you."

Humming, she heads back to the study. The music comes on again, blasting. Mina doesn't say anything, merely watches Crystal with confusion. Whenever Crystal's eyes meet Mina's, Crystal flashes a smile.

"What're you up to anyway?"

"What?"

Mina points to the knives in Crystal's hands.

Crystal is at a loss for words and it bothers her. "Um, uh, I thought I'd help...treat your mind." Putting her fists to her head Crystal mimics pulling something out and says, "Treat...treatment, you know?"

"Can you put those away?"

"Put what away?"

"The knives."

"Where?"

"Back in the kitchen."

"They didn't come from there. I bought them."

"What for?"

Again Crystal is at a loss for words and again it bothers her. Mina stares, confused, at the knives, then into Crystal's gleaming eyes. Crystal watches Mina's confusion grow. The knives shine.

"I'm going to change."

Crystal nods. She follows Mina to her room. When Mina tries to shut the door Crystal sticks the blade between the door and the jamb, preventing her. Mina cries out.

"I won't look," says Crystal, slipping into the room.

Mina's face is pale.

"It's okay. Don't worry. We'll just...talk." Crystal waves the knives.

Mina backpedals, scared. "I want to change first."

"I said go ahead." Crystal scrapes the door with the knives.

"Hey, don't do that. You're messing it up."

Crystal continues scraping the door.

"I told you not to do that."

Crystal laughs. "Hurry up and change."

Mina turns away, takes off her bathrobe, and puts on her panties. With an admiring sigh Crystal stares at her back and waist. Mina slowly clips her bra, pulls on a black sleeveless T-shirt, and then a white T-shirt with a deep V-neck over that, and then, just as slowly, takes a pair of jeans from her closet.

"Haven't seen those before."

"I bought them last week."

"Nice."

"So what do you want to talk about?"

Without saying anything Crystal cocks her head and looks at Mina with a languid expression.

"You look pretty."

"Will you please put down those knives?"

"Why? Do they scare you?"

No response.

"If I want to put them down I will. Let's go to the living room. Come on."

Mina heads haltingly toward the living room.

Crystal points her to the far end of the sofa. "You sit there, I'll sit here. Hey, don't be such a scaredy-cat. We'll just have ourselves a little chat."

"About what?"

"Oh, now I've forgotten. If only you wouldn't keep harping on me...."

"Are you threatening me for some reason? Is that what the knives are for?"

"The knives aren't the issue," says Crystal. And then she stabs the sofa.

Mina bounces up in shock. Taking in her reaction, Crystal cuts into the sofa more before pulling the knife out.

"Do you remember back in eighth grade when we were feeding pigeons in the park? We found a patch of beans, broke open one of the pods, and divided up the beans. I took mine home and planted them, but they all died."

"Why are you talking about that now?"

"It just came to mind and I figured why not. What's the matter? Should I not have said it?"

"You sound like you've gone nuts."

"How so?"

"I feel weird."

"About what?"

"Well…"

"I'm weird—that's what you've always told me."

"You *really* sound like you've gone nuts."

"Here we go again, you and your shrink."

"Why do you have such a problem with me mentioning Jung? And he's not a shrink."

"Then what was he? Tell me, Mina. I'm curious. I'd like to know. Anyway, you shouldn't talk to people like that. You're the one who's gone crazy. Not me. Crazy enough to quit school. And just look where you ended up—a school for weirdos."

"*You* shouldn't say things like that."

"Okay, here's a question: Why did you quit school? And why did you quit without even telling me first—you didn't say a word about it."

"Why should I? You're not my mom."

"You're right, I'm not. But I don't talk things over with my mom. I do with you, though."

"When? That's not true!"

"Yes, I have. Always."

"All right. So what if you do?"

Crystal sighs, glaring at Mina. "Why do you always make me repeat myself? It's giving me a sore throat. I'll ask you again: Why did you quit school, and why did you quit without talking to me about it first."

"You're… Are you trying to pick a fight with me?"

"No. I'm trying to talk."

"But listen to how you're talking to me."

"I'm talking normally."

"Ha!"

"Don't change the subject. Why did you quit school?"

"That's my business. It doesn't concern you."

"Just because it's your business it doesn't concern me?"

"Look, Crystal."

"Tell me."

"*You* tell *me*—what's the point of all this? It's okay. I'll understand. Did you have a fight with Minho? Did he dump you? Did he say he doesn't want to see you anymore?"

Crystal breaks out laughing. The laughter is exaggerated and offensive.

"If not that then what, damn it, what? What is it you want to talk about? What's on your mind? What's all this shit about a bean patch?"

"The bean patch isn't important."

"Then what is?"

"You and me."

"What about you and me! And how's that connected

with going crazy and buying kitchen knives! Crystal, why are you doing this? What did I do, anyway?"

"Frustrating, isn't it? Same for me. So chill out, I don't know why I'm doing this either. What I *do* know is I have to do it. I can't explain but I'm sure. I can feel it. That's why I wanted to go all the way back to the bean patch. But maybe that wasn't the start. Then what? Hmm. Maybe when we went to your auntie's place on Cheju? No, that's not it either... When we had sashimi rice bowls together three times a day for three days in a row. I felt like I was turning into a fish. What I really want to know is, did you drop out of school because of Pak Chiye?"

"Don't bring that up. I've told you a thousand times I don't want to talk about it. And don't keep mentioning her; she's not your pet."

"I will if I want to."

"Why?"

"Because I don't like her. I don't like her at all."

"Why not?"

"Because she killed herself, she made you quit school, she was a loser—I hate everything, everything about her. I hate her! I would have killed her myself but she beat me to it! So, what did you really know about Pak Chiye anyway?"

"A lot more than you do."

"Oh really?" Crystal sneers.

Mina responds slowly and deliberately: "Does it help you to feel like you're queen bitch when you're disrespectful of others...even of people who are dead?"

"No, I didn't say that to make myself feel like queen bitch; I can say that because I *am* queen bitch. And because I'm queen bitch, I *feel* like queen bitch. Don't get it turned around. And I'm not being disrespectful, I'm just telling you the way it is. You're the one being disrespectful. You make such a big deal out of her suicide, you make such a big deal out of your pain. *You're* the one who wants to look like queen bitch."

"Oh really? That's interesting. You sure can *talk*. Give it to me one more time, give me your best shot."

"Okay, fine, so you're mocking me again. You think you're better than me, don't you? Yeah, I know. You think I'm inferior to you. You don't have to say it—I already know. And yet you always smile, always act nice to me. You make me want to puke."

"Oh."

"You're scummier than chewing gum stuck to the sidewalk, cigarette butts, snotty Kleenex, shit flies on a watermelon rind, rotten fish guts, cockroaches, rusty nails, mercury, nuclear waste, Dioxin, MSG, PM10. You…you…you…are so fucking low class."

"*You're* the bad one."

"Yeah, I'm bad all right—don't I look like a scorpion with these things?"

"Will you stop talking shit and put those down! You're scaring me!"

"Then just fucking die."

"Is that what you want?"

Crystal nods.

"Why?"

"I won't pull the kind of shit you pulled when *you* die."

"I don't get it."

"Chiye died so you dropped out of school. You didn't go to class and you turned in a blank answer sheet for the final exam. Why would you do that? I got to thinking. You know, Mina, I don't like this either. It sounds like I'm obsessed with you, but that's not true. I don't like anyone. No one. And there's nothing I need. The thing is that I'm disgusted by you. I hate everything you have. Everything. And that's why I want to kill you. I can smell your rot and it scares me to even be near you. You're dirty, I'm clean, and I hate dirty things. You're dirty. You're an embodiment of everything that's dirty. I'm scared that all that scum will stick to me. I hate it. It makes me furious. And I think that with every year that's gone by you've gotten more and more rotten."

"Okay…I think I get it."

"You get what I'm saying?"

"I think you're mad because I didn't keep in touch. I didn't talk to you about it when I quit school. I left you out in the cold."

"So it's just that simple."

"But you're the one who started it, right? You rejected me first. Don't you remember? Well, I do. You rejected me. It was you. You. We're done; I already told you. What else do you want to know? We're done. So don't start now; it's too late. I don't want to talk to you anymore. We're through. Once and for all."

"No. It's not too late. We can change things." Crystal gets down on her knees and crawls toward Mina. She still has a knife in each hand. "No, Mina. It's not too late. There's still time. All you have to do is open your heart. Then we can go back to the way we were before." Suddenly, she's sobbing. "It's up to you. Please. Help me."

Mina is at a loss. Crystal looks to her with pitiful eyes full of tears. The knives horrify Mina.

"I told you," says Mina in a trembling voice. "I told you we're done."

Crystal opens her mouth wide but no sound escapes.

"I'm sorry," Mina says.

Crystal shakes her head, then suddenly she's on her feet, stomping on the floor.

"We're not done, you idiot! We've only just started!"

She paces quickly back and forth, mumbling: "IknewitI knewfromthestartIdidn'tlikeanythingaboutyouthefirsttime IsawyouIknewyouweregarbageIhatedyouyouweregarbage dirtyrottenyou'regarbagegarbageworsethangarbage. Worsethan garbage. WorsethangarbagegarbageandI'mgoingtokillyou."

"I'm sorry."

"That's garbage too. A garbage apology is garbage. You're garbage. You're everything I hate. I get it now. I've thought things over since our last argument. I've really done a lot of thinking. Why? I have everything. Just like you said, I have everything. So it's not about feeling inferior. It's about…I don't know, I feel sick. Like I might puke. One look at you and yuck! You should know one thing. I never felt inferior to you. Never. Never." Crystal shakes her head over and over again. "Then why would I kill you? I just don't know."

"I do."

"Tell me."

"For real?"

"Sure."

"Frankly, I never wanted to have to say this, but I need to be open—don't get upset. Crystal—the reason you turned out like this…you're self-centered. You think you can solve everything logically. But no. That's not possible. You can't. You just can't. To fix things you need something else. Something you just don't have. And trying to get it doesn't help. That's why things keep getting messed up for you. Why things don't work out your way. So, you get angry. But it never crosses your mind that you might be the problem. So, your anger keeps building. More and more—how can you find a fucking solution when you're just getting angrier? Crystal—there's only one solution: be kind.

"Just try to be kind, Crystal. From now on. Otherwise nothing's going to work out. See, you're already having trouble with it. Maybe you don't know what it's like to be kind. You don't accept that you have a problem. But that doesn't mean the problem is going away. The world is made by kind hearts. If you can't accept that, there's nothing we can do. That's the way the world works. The world isn't as fucked up as you think! It's okay to be sad when your friend dies. Not all of us want to tear others apart like you do. You probably don't believe it, but that's only because you still act young. But you'll learn. And you'll look back at how you were and feel ashamed. I wonder when you'll finally grow up. When? Will that day ever come? I don't know. There's *no way* you'll believe me now. You just have to figure it out for yourself, it's the only way. Unfortunately, there are more and more kids who are like you, and kids like you make the world a colder, harder place. And we forget what the world was like before. And it scares me. I'm so-so-so scared. I really am. I'm so scared, Crystal. You don't even understand why, do you? You probably wouldn't understand even if I laid it out for you. The world you see and the world I see are different. So kill me. Or don't. But no matter what you're making a big mistake."

With her tender voice and a kind gleam that lingers in her eyes, Mina talks like a mother to her wayward daughter.

Appalled by Mina's radiance, Crystal covers her mouth with one of the knives. "What the hell?!"

"That's right, Crystal. Put the knives down."

"Oh my god…all this time I've really, totally misunderstood."

Gently nodding, Mina extends her hand.

"All right…I get it…You're the devil. I was a bit confused till just now about whether you're really evil or not. I thought you might just be a little lamb in a devil's mask. It sure seemed possible. So I…I tricked you. I confused you with all that stuff about the bean patch and sashimi rice bowls. And you fell for it! And now I know for sure." Face lit by a smile, she looks up to the chandelier and shouts, "Yes!… Now I see. I see it clearly. I see your devil gleam. I see it. Ahhh. I am awesome. How did I get to be so awesome? So beautiful, so amazingly beautiful! You almost had me there—what an idiot I was. But I see that devil in your face, I see that devil gleam. How have you been able to hide it? You must have had a *devil* of a time. The world is made up of kind hearts…to you maybe. To a devil, evil is good and good is evil, right? Yes. I can see you can't be redeemed. You're really evil, evil through and through. And so you must die. You must, and I'll do it. I once thought you and I were the same. I must have been totally out of my mind. We're opposites. You're evil, I'm good. You're a devil, I'm an angel."

Crystal spreads her arms wide and flaps them like wings. Mina is speechless. Should she say something or not? All she can do is swallow.

"You're a devil because I believe you're a devil."

"Don't make me laugh—you're being lame."

"Is that why you're trembling?"

"Think about it. What if I marched into your place with a pair of knives…"

"Why do you keep avoiding the issue! Why! Why!" Crystal stomps, the knives flail in the air.

Mina's face betrays a mix of emotions, terror at the forefront.

"I'm not going to do it. I'm not going to…"

Mina's expression softens.

"Not yet anyway."

Mina's face hardens again.

Crystal watches Mina calmly. "Sorry, I didn't mean to interrupt.... You were saying?"

Mina's eyes pool with tears. "You know..." She blinks, and the tears spill down her cheeks. Shuddering, she puts a hand over her mouth. Her body reacts with shock and shame. Mentally she's lost all control. She's choking and words won't come, the tears continuing to fill her eyes, and she can't think straight. Crystal watches her tenaciously, waiting for her to speak. But Mina feels it not as waiting but as a threat. After all, Crystal has said she'll kill her, and she has a pair of knives. Mina's mind rejects it, but her trembling body reacts otherwise. She has to say something. Anything.

"You know...I know you and I are different in a lot of ways...but how could..." And then she breaks down, sobbing.

"Stop it, Mina. Or else I'll start bawling myself."

Mina shakes her head. Her tears fall on the floor. "Can I get a tissue?" she mumbles in a teary voice, pointing to the box of tissue beneath the TV. Crystal nods.

Mina staggers toward the tissue box. Then she suddenly races to the far wall and snatches the intercom's receiver. Pushing the red button, she screams for help. Crystal watches, motionless, not comprehending at first. Mina blanches when she realizes the intercom's not working. Crystal gets up and walks toward her. Mina runs to her parents' room with Crystal close behind. Before Mina can shut the door, Crystal blocks it from closing with the blade of one of the knives. Mina screams and lets go of the doorknob. Crystal kicks the door open. Mina throws a chair at her. It hits Crystal in the left shoulder before thumping to the floor. With a bestial shriek

Crystal stabs at the legs of the chair with the knife in her left hand. The blade snaps off. Crystal throws the broken knife to the floor and curses. Then she inches toward Mina, the other knife held high in her right hand. Wailing, Mina throws pillows at Crystal. She closes her eyes. Nothing happens. She keeps wailing, but nothing happens. Her wailing slowly dies down. She opens her eyes just enough to see Crystal, knife lowered, watching her, composed.

"Let's go back to the living room and talk. Come on."

Mina kneels on the bed, hands together in supplication. "Crystal, please."

"We're not done talking yet."

"Please."

Crystal scowls at her.

"Please." Wiping her tears, Mina eases off the bed.

"No one can hear you scream. You ought to know that. Try to run off again and I'll slice your arm open."

Mina goes back to the far end of the living room sofa. Crystal returns to where she was before. They regard each other. Then Crystal stands and walks over to Mina, whose face is a mask of fear.

"Why? What are you doing? I'm not going to run away."

"But you did." Crystal positions her knife over Mina's thigh.

"Look, Crystal, I screwed up. I won't do it again."

"What do you prefer, just a stab wound or do you want to die now?"

"Huh? What? Are you…?"

"Don't stall; it won't work."

"I won't run away again. I promise."

Crystal nods. Mina forces a grin. They look at each other for a time. The silence ends when, without warning, Crystal plunges the knife into Mina's thigh. Mina shrieks and clutches her leg. Wiping the glistening blade on her pants, Crystal is about to go back to her place on the sofa when Mina grabs her wrist and tries to snatch the knife. Crystal flails, swiping the knife back and forth and cutting them both, before kicking Mina in her bleeding thigh as hard as she can. Mina tumbles screaming to the floor.

Crystal sits down again. Mina stays splayed on the floor, not moving.

"Get up, you fucking bitch! I know you're not dead!"

But Mina doesn't move. Crystal has cuts on both of her arms. She examines them, scowling. Mina is still not moving. Crystal stands over her with the bamboo salt. Ripping the bag open, she dumps the salt on Mina's thigh and rubs it in with the sole of her foot. Shrieking, Mina grabs Crystal by the ankle. When Crystal tries to jerk her foot free, Mina bites the ankle. With her other foot, Crystal kicks Mina in the stomach. She keeps kicking until Mina lets go. Then she returns swiftly to her place on the sofa.

"Sit."

"Just kill me."

"I don't want to."

"Okay, Crystal, then let's stop. I'll pretend that all of this never happened. It never happened."

Crystal stares intently at Mina's blood-soaked pant leg. Groaning, Mina tries to wipe the salt from the gash in her leg.

"Hey, don't do that. Sodium is a disinfectant, you know."

Mina glares at Crystal.

Crystal gives her a wide grin. "Where did we leave off?"

Mina shakes her head.

"Fine, I don't remember either. So we'll just start all over again."

Mina gives her a pleading look.

"The bean patch, I remember that. You too, right?"

"What I want to know is *why* are you doing this?" Mina's feeble voice trails off.

"We'll get there. We've got lots of time. Minho's not going to be here till late."

"Minho?"

"Yeah, Minho. This is all because of him." Crystal gives Mina a knowing smile.

"I don't believe anything you say anymore."

"Keep it up and your arm's next."

"Go ahead."

"Why not?"

Crystal gets up and approaches Mina. Mina holds out her hands to fend her off.

"Crystal, stop it. Why would you want to cut my arm? Don't do this. Don't. I'm telling you, I don't understand why you're doing this. I thought we were friends?" Tears flow from Mina's eyes again.

"Well, like I said, I don't know either. So why don't we put our heads together and see if we can figure it out?"

Mina drops her head and sobs.

"But it all comes down to you in the end. It's all because of you. You've done wrong so I'm going to kill you. Somewhere you screwed up your life. Because you've lived a screwed-up life. And that's the reason. The only reason."

"But you said before it was because I disgust you! You said I was garbage!"

"Whatever. Why's it so important to have a reason, anyway? Are you alive because you have a reason to be? You don't die because you have a reason. Everybody dies without a reason. You will. Me too. You might not like it, but there's not much you can you do about it, right? That's life."

Holding the knife so she can see her reflection in the blade, Crystal smooths her hair back.

"Primp all you want, it won't help your face, you low-life bitch."

"Your dear brother gave me the okay. He gave me permission to kill you."

"Crazy bitch."

"He hates you. So he said to go ahead."

"You think you can hurt me by talking like that?"

"Yeah."

"Then bring it on, all the way. See if you can hurt me."

"You're being ridiculous, Mina. Look at your leg. It's bleeding, see? Are you telling me it doesn't hurt? What for? Anyway, I'm not here to injure you, I'm here to kill you."

"Go fuck yourself."

"Hey, no swearing! No swearing! I told you!" Crystal gets up and looks toward the chandelier melodramatically. "Hey, Mina. You want to sing? I do."

And the next moment Crystal is singing.

> *Minho's little sister's friend is Crystal!*
> *Crystal's friend's brother is Minho!*
> *Mina's friend's boyfriend is my boyfriend!*
> *My boyfriend's girlfriend's friend's mom is my mom!*
> *My mom's son's girlfriend's boyfriend's little sister is my*
>   *daughter!*
> *My daughter's mom's daughter's big brother's girlfriend's*
>   *friend is Crystal!*
> *Crystal!*
> *Yeah Crystal!*
> *Yeah Mina!*

Yeah Minho!
Yeahhhh!
Minho! Let's hear it for Minho! And Mina!
Yeah, yeah, yeah Crystal!

"Eh? Not bad, right? I thought it up just now! Now it's your turn. Get up! Sing! Be happy! Hey, why's your face so purple?"

"I'm cold."

"Of course. Maybe it's too much for you to sing in your condition. But it's okay. That's how you become an adult. Way to go, Mina—congratulations on growing up, Mina. There's only one problem: I hate grown-ups. *I'm* not going to be injured. *I'm* not going to be in pain. Oh, what a smart girl I am, what a fantastic student I am. If people only knew how smart, they'd be *amazed*. Oh, how sad. Oh, how happy. That asshole dean of students hates me because I'm smarter than him, that's why. How I wish I was crazy, a total nutcase. Then no one would bother me anymore, they'd all leave me alone   oh, I think I've maybe really   gone mad."

She shakes her head and shrugs emphatically.

"How come that asshole hates me? Mina, do you know? Mina? What's up? Why won't you look at me?" She shakes Mina. By reflex Mina shoots out an arm and pushes Crystal's hand aside. She looks like a monster, her face contorted with hate, horror, and disgust.

"Mina, you ought to see yourself. Don't make that face, it makes you look so ugly…I can't believe it. You really disappoint me. Why can't you try to look beautiful? You never looked like this before. Mina, don't disappoint me. Because if you do, I might really kill you."

"I'm…cold."

"Ahh…you know, out of all the kids, it's *me* that asshole

hates—I don't know why. One day he said to me, nice and quiet-like: 'I've seen lots of kids like you before.' Oh was I shocked!... Let's try English: *How can I say...what can I say...I was...to...tally...damaged....*"

And then in Korean again, she says, "Why would he say that? *What* was he talking about? What was he trying to say? There are lots of kids like me? How could that be possible? It's *im*possible. How am I supposed to believe that? But I couldn't stop thinking about it. How could I? I...everybody knows how smart I am—three years in a row I was voted most likely to succeed. I know it. I know I'm special. I know that better than anyone. *How* could he say that to a person like me? I'm going to get even with him."

Mina trembles with her arms crossed tight. "My leg hurts. No...I can't feel it anymore."

"Yeah. I know. It hurts, right? I know! Do you think I don't know?! Oh...sorry...I'm too worked up, sorry."

"My poor leg."

"You need to die because you respect grown-ups. You do, don't you? You love your mom and you love your dad. You love Minho. And your teachers. All of them. Your aunts, your uncles, your grandmothers, even your aunts by marriage. It's because of trash like you that the world is falling apart. How can you respect these adults? While you kiss up to them they're stealing what's most important from you and you don't have a clue. They're stealing it all, they leave nothing. Nothing except dirty, rotting wounds. It's horrifying, don't you think? And that's the life of a grown-up! And you *respect* it! Because of people like you the world keeps getting dirtier. Do you get it? You need to know. You ought to feel guilty. You should cry and beg forgiveness. You need to lick the bathroom floor in apology. You need to bow down and get

trampled on. You smell like B.O. Get away from me. I hate
you. Do you really think I'm acting out of bullshit feelings—
an inferiority complex, loss, some bullshit like that? *Wrong.*
I don't care about *complexes.* They're totally unimportant. I
don't feel them. Sometimes I even scare myself. That has to be
why the asshole hates me. And that's why I hate people like
you who feel everything. And it's because of all those bullshit
feelings that you respect grown-ups and mope around over
your friend's death—right? And it's because you waste your
time on those bullshit feelings that the world is getting shit-
tier. You're wasting everything that's good about you. And I
hate waste. You're a perfect example of how emotions mess
things up. How do you parade around all those stupid emotions? How did you come up with them? *Where* did you learn
them? Did someone *make* you learn them? We don't need
them in this world. People like you are harmful. That's why
you ended up in a stupid alternative school—you're a loser.
The world wants people like me. *And* it wants people like me
to kill people like you. Nobody will say a thing, because I'm
perfect! I'm not bragging, I don't *have* to brag, because I'm
already there, and we both know it. It's impossible to be better
than me. It's a big world and there are a lot of great people,
but no one's better than me. I can *feel* it. I work myself to
death, all the time. I can be proud; I can feel like I should get
what I deserve. And the world acknowledges my efforts. But
what about you? What were *you* doing while I was working
so hard? You were drowning in sorrow about Chiye, that's
what. Let's assume that was real, though I have my doubts.
You did well, you're commendable, Mina, you're outstanding.
Your skill, your talent, they're out of this world. But all of that
is useless. The world wants a person like me, people want a life
like mine. They, uh, how can I put it…they *encourage* a person

like me, they *recommend* a life like mine. But you? How can you live in a place like this trying to be as wise and calm as a Buddha. Look where you live. Whose idea was all this? *Look* at what you have here. You want to be a noble family? You long to be European, don't you? Well guess what. This place is garbage. And this garbage has made garbage out of you. You read books by Europeans and take European trips, you live in a European-style house and eat European food in your European dining room, you go to a European alternative school to get a European education—I love Europe, too, isn't that what this is all about? Those quaint old countries with their cheese, you love them. You think you can be European just by imitating them. You think European blood will flow in your veins, that you'll be charged with some European energy. Does that sound normal to you? And *you* want to tell me *I'm* crazy? It's obvious that I'm way more normal than you are. What the world wants, and what I want from the world that wants me, is normalcy—not abnormality. And the way I see it, you're abnormal. You don't make sense. How can you be satisfied with all this stuff you have when you don't even notice it? How can you be content with that innocent-looking smile on your face?"

Crystal's cheeks are blazing and she's shivering with rage. She *has* to do something. She takes the Bohemian crystal vase from the coffee table and hurls it at the TV. It arcs through the air and shatters the screen. This only feeds her rage. All she can do is walk in circles and scream, and then she glares at Mina.

"Why don't you answer me?"

Mina is shivering, too, her cheeks streaked white by dried tears. Her thigh blooms in an ugly mélange of colors, mostly hidden by her jeans.

"So you're saying... Ahh, it's cold. So cold. I, I, ahh... fuck. So you're saying I should feel sorry for living in a place like this? I should be living in poverty if I'm going to go to an alternative school? Seriously, what are you saying, what's your point, what do you mean, seriously, you haven't given me one decent explanation of why you're threatening to kill me. Seriously, Crystal! Seriously, this is ridiculous. What do you want from me? What the fuck do you want? What?! I'm cold. Crystal...I'm begging you. Please. Please. My leg hurts so bad it feels like it's coming off, and then it feels like it's not there anymore, and my arm is numb too. I'm cold. I'm dizzy. I'm going to throw up. I'm going to throw up."

"...What are we going to do with you?... You don't understand anything I've... Amazing.... Unbelievable." Crystal's mouth hangs open in a shocked look. But the next moment her face turns icy. "Look, Mina, I really feel sorry for you. You're so messed up in the head. What else can I do but...? Why are you smiling?"

"Because you're funny."

"I don't love you anymore. And I've decided to kill you. I'm not sure which one came first. But it's true that I once loved you and it's true that I've now decided to kill you. Go ahead and smile—it's better than crying. I want you to die with a smile on your face. I'd hate to see you crying then. I really tried to remain hopeful. I really tried to change...to change you....

"Ahhhhhhhhhhhhhhhh....

"Mina.

"I'm going to have it all. I'm going to take everything I need, and I'm going to get rid of anything I don't need. I'm not going to leave anything behind. Am I scaring you? Or do you just think I'm funny? You're shivering. You're pale. Your leg's still bleeding. Wow, look at all that blood. I can't believe you've been bleeding all this time. You've lost a lot of blood but you mostly look the same. It's amazing, I'll have to weigh you after you die. Tell me, what do you think of me? I've always wondered, but you've never really told me. It's strange, but I guess I know why. You dissed me, you know, and today you'll pay the price. I worry about what others think of me. You look so sad. It's because you're a reject. Oh, I get so frustrated looking at you. I don't want to think about it. I'm gonna kill you. I'm gonna kill you. I'm gonna kill you. Mina? Can you believe it? Do you believe I can? Do you? You don't. I don't either. And…that's why…that's why…oh hell, there's so much I want to say, but I'll skip it and just kill you instead."

Suddenly a thin white ray of light is emitted from Crystal's brain. She feels as if a large hammer has tapped her in the back of her head. She sees the light glinting off the knife blade and she flinches. She looks around and all she sees are sleek surfaces reflecting the light.

"Who turned on all these lights? Why's it so bright?"

Her wide eyes come to rest on Mina. She stares, her face empty. Mina is a mass of glittering, blinding molecules. The molecules move on wisps of air, coming apart and reforming, and within them Crystal sees Mina's blood and bones and flesh. Mina's expressions, gestures, and movements no longer seem human. Instead, Crystal is aware of a kind of flow of constantly changing geometrical patterns. And she watches Mina's blood-red heart, previously hidden beneath her skin and clothing. The pumping is beautiful.… Even Crystal can sense that. It's so red, charged with blood, forever moving… plump, warm, strong, and pliable. It occurs to her that she could close her fist around it and *splosh*. She slowly lifts her hand…then lowers it before approaching Mina. Mina gets up. The glittering molecules trickle off of her into a pile on the floor. Crystal, smiling faintly, can't keep her eyes from the trickle.

"Where are you going? Sit. It's all coming back. I remember it all. All the time I've spent with you. The happy days and the shitty days. I think I'll keep them. It's nice to have good memories. Look at those big old stars, look at the moon. Let's pray. Come on. Where are you? Pray. Let's do what's most urgent first. Then we'll think over what's next. In our case, goodbyes. What are you doing? Come on, it's time to say goodbye. I bet you wish you were in your closet now. I went inside your closet once, for you. Let's go get in your closet together. Then if anyone asks Crystal what she did for dear, departed Mina, she can say she went into her closet with her. Hey, that's it! That takes care of everything! We're all set, then. Right? Are you with me? You don't have to answer, just nod. All right. Come on. Nod. That's right. If you can do it, I won't kill you."

Mina nods.

"All right. Excellent. Thank you so much. As for anybody else—let them think whatever they want. Let them. I'm normal. Normal enough. I'm not crazy. I'm in my right mind, right? Right? Then nod. Right? Just nod and I won't kill you."

Mina clutches the sofa with both hands, trembling. Tears run from Crystal's eyes.

"No. No crying. Don't feel sad. Don't be sad, Crystal. Be stoic when I kill you. Nod for me, Mina. Nod your head. You're still alive. You don't want to die, right? So show me. Show it. Ask me not to kill you. Beg for your life. Come on. Why can't I feel you anymore? Come on. Tell me why you want to live. I need to be *moved*. Please. Why don't I feel sorry for you? Why do I feel you're worth about as much as a pencil? You're nothing, are you? Right? Tell me. Tell me there doesn't need to be a reason to kill, just like there's no reason to die, okay? Tell me. Nod. Can't you shiver any more than that? Mina, I don't have a reason. Nothing. That's me. I've lived without one till now and I'll go on the same way. Don't ask me. Don't ask me why. Got it? Then let's hear you say something."

Mina's still in motion. The molecules flow and pile, gather and disperse. Crystal can't believe what she's seeing. She closes her eyes tight and opens them again. They're still there. In order to believe it she stabs Mina. Eyes closed, she thrusts as deeply as possible, up to the hilt, feeling the blade move through Mina's body, her blood vessels and muscles, hearing it enter and then leave her body. Her mouth opens into a faint smile. Blood spurts from severed arteries, splattering her T-shirt and leaving wedge-shaped splotches sprayed on the windows and an exclamation-point smear on one of the peacock's wings. A thick rivulet creeps along the floor. Mina's screams and the noise of the metal working through flesh are impossibly distant; Crystal still can't believe it. Looking at Mina's gaping mouth, she keeps stabbing. But she still can't believe it.

"My head's been killing me, and it's because of…you. All this time…I couldn't do anything and it's because of… you. You were the obstacle. I was always looking behind me, always thinking, always wondering, and it was because of… you. You were always figuring out ways to lie to me. Why, Mina? I want to cry but I'll smile instead. Crying is for losers. For people who deserve to be ridiculed. It makes things complicated, it turns you into more garbage, you become the obstacle. I've removed the last obstacle and now I'm running. Crystal. Running to the finish line. I, Crystal, am running.

Run, Crystal! Win, Crystal. You're not breathing but don't forget. I won't. Okay? Then give me a nod. Give me a nod and say yes."

Blood-draped Mina slides to the floor. Her limp ankle is fair and sleek, no longer a collection of molecules dispersing and reforming. Crystal backpedals in fear. The background quickly dims. Far away, Madonna's song. Crystal sings a song of her own:

> *But she bows her head*
> *But she bows her head*
> *We can see her face no more*
> *We're sad but we won't cry*
> *Won't cry, we're sad*
> *Getting sadder and sadder*
> *The day is dark and we can't see anything*
> *We see nothing, nothing*
> *That's why we're glad, we're glad*

"I'll give you an example of something everybody says. Here it is: 'You get ahead by stepping on your friends' backs.' Or 'I'm feeling smothered.' Metaphors, right? Nothing to them. I need something real. *I* step on your hand and *I* crush it. No metaphor. I actually step on your hand. What if I actually did that? What would happen? What, really, is the difference between actually doing those things and doing them metaphorically? Now I know. There's no difference. I don't feel anything. There you are dead, but I don't feel a thing. I feel you less, now that you're dead, than when you were alive. And that's a great ending."

Crystal strokes Mina. Suddenly the world silently shrinks. And with its cheerful, three-note warble the front door opens. Crystal looks toward the door. It's Minho.

"Hey, Minho. I did it."

She greets him with a bright smile.

Minho looks at her and he smiles too. The two smiling faces are like mirror images. Heads down, they examine the corpse lying between them, and when they look up they're still smiling. One corpse. Two smiles. Incalculable darkness.